THE GRANT BROTHERS SERIES BOOK 2

KATHI S. BARTON

WCP

World Castle Publishing, LLC
Pensacola, Florida

Copyright © by Kathi S. Barton 2011
ISBN: 9781937085438
Library of Congress Catalogue Number 2011931977

First Edition World Castle Publishing, LLC July 15, 2011
http://www.worldcastlepublishing.com

Cover Artist: Karen Fuller
Editor: Brieanna Robertson

Dedication

This book I dedicate to the women in my life - Daniy, Dale, and Wendy. I love you all very much. Also, I know too damned much about your sex lives. Next time you want to share, please remember these three little letters: TMI.

Also to Brieanna Robertson, my editor extraordinaire. You're great at editing and your wonderful funny comments have been so much fun. I'm so excited to be working with someone who 'gets' me. Thanks for making both Nickolas and Devin readable. You're the best.

And finally to Karen Fuller, Owner of World Castle Publishing. You took a chance with me and my books. I will forever be grateful to you. I know that we will have a long and wonderfully fulfilling relationship.

Kathi S. Barton

~*Chapter 1*~

Ronnie Frey pulled out her books and sat them on one of the tables in the back of Bob's Diner where she worked. It was just after three o'clock in the morning and she hoped that no one else would be in the diner tonight. Well, except for the cops who came by for a cup of fresh coffee and to check up on her. They seemed to think she needed someone to look over her, and she generally let them.

When the SUV pulled up outside at a little after four, she frowned. Walking over to the coffee maker, she pushed the button to start a new pot. When the bell chimed over the door, she turned to look at the newcomers and her heart skipped several beats before she trusted herself to speak.

Four of the most gorgeous men she had ever seen walked in playing and jabbing at the one who was, by far, the most beautiful man she had ever seen. *Christ*, she thought. Why did every beautiful man have to be gay, and why did four of them have to descend on her at once? It was enough to make a woman want to give up on ever finding true love and join a nunnery. Shaking herself mentally on that morose thought, she turned to the men and smiled.

1

"Have a seat anywhere. I'll be right with you. Coffee will be about three more minutes," she told them when they paused in their laughter to look at her.

They picked a booth about midway back and sat two by two. Ronnie took them their glasses of water and silverware and walked away. They had not picked up their menus yet, so she went back to her book and marked her page. When she was finished, the pot had finished brewing the coffee, so snagging four cups and the pot, she went over to the table.

"Coffee? The cream is fresh. I'll bring it to you if you need it. Have you decided what you want yet?" She sat the pot on the table behind her, pulled out her pad and pen and looked at them expectantly.

The one they had been teasing looked at her with what seemed to her like anger. Ronnie was surprised by it, but said nothing as she waited. She knew she didn't know him. Ronnie was certain of that. She'd remember a man who looked like him.

"Well, I'm not sure, Ronnie," he said as he looked pointedly at her name tag. "We usually get something to tell us what our choices are before someone comes around to take our order. Most waitresses bring menus before she tries to find out what we want to eat. Maybe you're new to this, but that's usually how it's done."

She looked at him and wanted to hit him, but knew that she could not. But her temper got the better of her mouth and she let it have free rein. Sometimes, that was just as lethal.

"Well, stupid old me. Let me get them for you." She pushed her pad and pen back into her pocket, leaned over him and the other man across from him, and plucked the menus out of the holder on the table. Making a huge production of it, she handed each man their menu and gave the man who had spoken his last. "I don't know why I thought you'd look before you stuck your foot in your mouth, sir. But, hey, that's the way it's usually done around here." She picked up the pot and turned to leave with a muttered "jackass" under her breath.

There was a sudden bark of laughter from the table as she headed to the kitchen after depositing the pot at the coffee maker. They must have heard her, not that she had been trying to be that quiet, but still...her hands shook as she stood there in front of the stove.

From the hours of three in the morning until seven-thirty when the breakfast crowd started coming in, Ronnie was the only one in the restaurant. She waited on anyone who ventured in and then cooked whatever they wanted. Usually, it was just coffee, but on occasion, she had to cook something.

When she felt she had a rein on her temper again, she went back to the men at the table.

"You ready to order?" Her voice was clipped, but at this point, she did not care.

The guy in the back smiled at her and ordered. "I'll have the Trucker's Special, eggs over easy and wheat toast. I would also like orange juice, please large." He had a smile that would melt most women's hearts. Too bad the man with him did not own one—a heart or a smile.

"How you want your steak, sir? And OJ is included, or you can have grapefruit juice. I have them both."

"OJ, thanks. And can the cook do Pittsburg rare? If so, that's what I want."

Nodding, she watched as he tucked his menu back in the holder and then the next guy ordered the same, including the steak. The third guy wanted his eggs scrambled and his steak just plain rare and he took the rest of the menus and put them away as well. That left the jerk. Everyone turned to look at him.

3

"If I order something, are you going to have the cook spit in my food, or are you going to drop it on the floor first?" She was sure he was just as mad at her as she was at him, but frankly, she did not care. She was pissed.

"You'll never know, will you? What do you want? Or were you waiting for me to turn the pages for you? Or do the waitresses where you come from just read your tiny mind for you and order everything just perfectly?"

The men with him laughed again and she flushed. It was not like her to be nasty to a customer, but he had rubbed her the wrong way.

"Christ, you always this nice to people who tip you, or is it just me? I'll take the Trucker's Special, Pittsburg rare, over easy, wheat toast and OJ."

She did not answer. She was afraid of what might spill from her lips. It was on the tip of her tongue to tell him off, and then throw him out, but she needed this job. She could study as long as the customers received good service, plus it paid for some of the outrageous prices of her law books.

Going to the table again, she topped off their cups and freshened their waters. Leaning down to the jerk, she whispered in his ear, "It's all you, baby," and went to the kitchen. His hiss of breath was all she heard as the door closed behind her, the arrogant bastard.

It took her fifteen minutes to fix the breakfasts and she was pilling it onto a tray when the bell rang, signaling the door opening. Great, she thought. They were leaving without paying. Tommy Bob, the owner with his mother, was going to be pissed. She was relieved when she heard Officer Roger Timpkin shout it was him, not to hurry. She finished putting the platters on the tray and picked it up, grabbing a tray jack on her way out the door.

Coming through the door, she noticed that Roger was at the counter drinking his usual cup of coffee, and he and the men were talking. She did not bother with what they were saying. She was too busy trying to balance the tray of food, juices, and other things to care.

She set the tray down and passed out their food, setting it before them. Pulling a bottle of catsup and steak sauce from her back jean pockets, she set them on the table and went to get the coffee pot. Ronnie noticed that Roger had started a new pot and took the old one to the men with a pot of butter and one of honey.

"Everything all right? There are fresh biscuits ready to come out in about six minutes, and I'll bring them out. If you all don't need anything, I'll be over there." She pointed to the back of the restaurant and went back to her books after setting the timer close to her.

When the timer rang, she pulled the hot bread from the oven and, putting a baker's dozen in a basket, dropped it off at the table with another round of juice and coffee. She topped off Roger's cup and sat back down. She was never much for small talk with customers and, other than asking if they needed anything else, she did not say much. Ronnie hated to be bothered when she went out, so tried to do the same for her customers.

Sometimes she got caught up in her reading and had learned to set a timer while studying for ten minute intervals when someone was in the restaurant. Roger sitting down across from her had her look up in surprise. He looked at her strangely then glanced back at the four men.

"Want me to hang out for a while? Never seen them men before—don't trust them. They're from the city and could mean trouble for you."

Ronnie sighed. It had been like this since she was a teenager and, working here, everyone thought she was frail and helpless. She was hardly either. At five feet ten inches, she towered over most men she knew and she held a black belt in karate. Then there was the gun strapped to her ankle and the other in her book bag. She carried a concealed weapons license and was a marksman on the firing rang. Few people messed with her when they found out she did not have the temperament for stupidity and was armed to boot.

"Nah, I can handle them. They're just a bunch of stupid men out with their dates. I think I'm safe from them. But thanks. I appreciate it."

He left a few minutes later, but she noticed that he stopped by the table before leaving and spoke to the guys. Gabbing up the pot, hopefully for the last time, she went to clear and give them their check.

"If you tell me who's with whom, I'll divide up the check for you," she told them as she started away with the dirty plates.

The man in the back, the one with the nice smile, told her he would take care of it and reached out for the bill she had already written up. It was not totaled, but she would do that at the cash register. She noticed that jerk was gone.

She took Spencer Grant's credit card and went to cash him out. He followed her to the register. His smile really was nice and she wondered fleetingly if he smiled like that for everyone.

"He's not usually such a prick. Okay, yeah he is, but he's usually nicer to pretty women than he was tonight. I'm sorry," he told her when she handed him his slip of paper to sign.

"I've dealt with worse. Don't let it bother you. You have a safe trip out." She started to turn away to clean up, but he stopped her.

"Miss, are you the only person here? The cop hinted that you were and made it a point to let us know that he and his men go by here frequently. He also said you carry a gun. You know it's not safe, regardless if you're armed or not. Someone could do a lot of damage to you in a short amount of time. You should tell your boss he'll be responsible if anything happens to you." He grinned to take some of the sting out of what he was saying, she was sure. "Where do you carry that thing anyway?"

Ronnie lifted her pant leg and showed him her ankle holster. He smiled and she felt its warmth all the way across the restaurant. When she turned back, she ran right into the arms of her jerk. He grabbed her before she fell over the chair and her body pressed hard against his.

Her body felt infused with heat and his scent. He smelled expensive and warm. Before she could stop herself, she buried her nose into his neck and inhaled. When he pulled her away from him and stared at her, she flushed with embarrassment. What the hell was wrong with her? She jerked back farther from him.

Taking another step back, she heard the man at the counter call, "Devin, come on, we need to get back," and she fled toward the kitchen.

~~~

Devin and his brothers got into the car and started off. He was not driving this leg of the journey home from their parents' house and was glad because he was not sure he could concentrate very well.

Ronnie. He did not know what had made him be especially mean to her, but he had. And he had to smile when

7

she did not back down from him like most women did. He found that he liked that. When women found out what he did for a living and who he was, they tended to fawn all over him.

Devin had had a shitty day. First, he had lost his case. It was not the first one he had, nor would it be his last, but it was one thing in the long line of his day. Then he had gotten a ticket on top of wrecking his new car. Margo Hemmingway had called while he had been waiting on the tow truck to come collect him and his totaled car to tell him that she was engaged and could not be his date for the annual charity dinner in two weeks. The two of them had remained friends after they had stopped dating about three years ago and she had been his date to his mother's charity event every year since. He was glad she was engaged. He was starting to feel weird vibes from her and he did not like it.

As the miles passed by, he thought of Ronnie's body pressed to his and nearly moaned out loud. She was tall but she still tucked nicely under his chin, and when she nuzzled his neck, he thought his cock would explode. Right now, he was harder than he had been in a long while and shifted to adjust himself against his too tight pants.

He had looked at her books when she had been busy with Spencer at the front on his way back from the men's room. Law books spread out all over the table and neat notes filled a spiral notebook still open over one of them. She had to be in her last year—close to finishing, he thought, and smiled when he thought of the huge tip he had slipped under her books. He knew how expensive books were, especially law books, and hoped she would put her hundred dollars to good use. Smiling to himself, he realized he needed to find himself a date and soon if pretty little waitresses made him so hard he ached.

~*Chapter 2*~

Class ran over an hour and she had missed the bus to the Grant Building. When she finally opened the doors to the huge thing, she was relieved that their heat was on. Her feet were cold and her hands felt frozen. She walked up to the security counter and smiled at the man sitting there. She had no reason to take her crappy mood out on him.

"Hi, my name is Ronnie Frey and I was wondering if I could speak to Mr. Grant, please? I don't have an appointment, but I have something I'd like to return to his friend. It won't take a minute."

"Do you know which Grant you wanted to see? There are three working in this building and three more spread out all over the city."

Ronnie noticed the very beautiful woman coming in with a stroller with a set of twins in it. She smiled. Cute kids and puppies always made her grin. Not that she ever wanted any, but they were still a source of entertainment.

"No, I don't...Wait! Spencer. His first name was Spencer. I'm not sure which man was his date, but he would know him, I would think. I promise you, I just want to return something to the jer...one of their dates."

"Date, ma'am? I don't think I know..." He looked over at the lady, confusion written all over his face. When Ronnie looked at her, the woman looked ready to burst with barely concealed humor. Weird.

"I'll take her up, David. Maybe Nickolas can clear this up. Come on, Miss Frey, did you say? Let's see who you need to talk to."

Ronnie was confused and a little wary of the woman who motioned her into the elevator ahead of her. When the woman leaned down and took one of the little boys from the stroller and handed him to Ronnie, she held him far away from her without dropping him.

"He won't hurt you. Just tuck him closer and he'll be fine. I'm Morgan, by the way."

"Ronnie. I don't know anything about kids, lady. Maybe you should take it back. It might cry or something." Though it did not look like it would, it just stared at her with the greenest eyes Ronnie had ever seen.

"He's a little boy not an 'it,' and if he cries, he cries. Just tuck him in like this." Ronnie looked over at the woman and marveled how she got the other one to cling to her hip and neck like that, but did not bring hers any closer to her. They both seemed to be fine just where he was.

When the elevator doors opened, there stood one of the men from last night. He had been sitting next to the jerk and she figured he was his date. Shoving "it," err...the little boy back at its stroller, Ronnie advanced on the man, poking him in the chest with the money clutched in her hand.

"You tell your lover boy that I do not want his charity. The nerve of that ass... I've been making it on my own for some time now and will continue to do so for a while longer. Take this and tell him to stick it where the sun doesn't shine or where ever. Have a nice life." She turned quickly and stepped back into the elevator and pushed the button several times to go down before the doors finally closed. She saw the man holding the money with one hand and looking at her as if she was insane.

When the elevator opened again, she walked into the lobby and stormed out of the building and right into the blistering cold afternoon. Damn it, she should have gone to pee first. Tucking down her head, she made her way home – all six flipping blocks.

~~~

Morgan was still laughing when Nick took his son from her. He was holding onto the money and when he looked at his wife, he knew there was no hope of getting anything from her just yet. He tried to wait until she calmed down, but he thought he would be waiting for a while and decided to chance it.

"Would you please tell me why the waitress from last night is accusing me of having a lover? A male lover, at that, and telling me to tell him she doesn't want his charity?"

He thought he had been very reasonable, but apparently, Morgan thought he was hysterical and she laughed all the harder. His sons thought she was funny, too, and started to giggle with her. Nick did not get her at times like this.

Nick set his son on the floor and went to unstrap his brother. He loved these little guys and loved it when Morgan brought them to work to see him. When they were both crawling around the office, he pulled her into his arms for a deep, sensual kiss. It had the desired effect. She stopped laughing, but now he wanted her.

They had been married almost two years now and he still could not get enough of her. He forgot why he needed her attention until he saw the money in his hand.

"Could you please tell me why Ronnie believes I have a lover, and why would he be giving her charity? And just so we're clear, any lover of mine would not be a spend thrift, especially to leave a hundred dollars as a tip. Why, I don't believe the whole bill came to thirty dollars."

"Of course he wouldn't. Now, the real question is, why did she think it was charity, and who were you with when this charity occurred?" Nick knew she was making fun of him, but he could not figure out how, and decided to let it slide — for now.

"Remember the little diner I told you about? Well, she was the...Devin!" When Morgan looked at him confused, he hurried on. "Devin was in a really bad mood and didn't want to stop, but Spence and Jamie were hungry, and you know me. I can eat anytime. Anyway, Devin started in with her. He was nasty about the menus. But damned if she didn't give it right back to him, called him a jackass — under her breath, but we heard her. We ordered and he just kept it up, asked her if she was gonna have the cook spit in his food or something. Come to find out this cop came in to check on her and he told us — actually, he warned us that he and his men came in regularly and checked up on her. He said he had our plate number and all. Turns out she cooked our food and served us too. He told us she was working her way through law school. Devin came out last so I bet he was the one who tipped her. I have to call him and tell him." He moved over to the phone when Morgan stopped him.

"No! Wait. I'd love to see his face when you tell him she thinks he's gay. I don't think he'll have an issue with it, but I want to see his face. Maybe he left the money for other reasons. He did just break up with that bitch, didn't he?"

"Nah, not Devin. I don't think he was actually seeing...what's her name, but she was his date for the charity thing. I think that was a little of his pissy-ness last night. I don't think he's really ready to pick up with another woman right now. It's too soon even for Devin."

Nick had just picked up his phone to call his brother when he came into the office after a short knock.

"You really need to get yourself a better receptionist. I'm not sure, but I think this one is the dumbest one yet. Hello, Morgan. How's my favorite sister-in-law?" Devin was just bending to pick up Anthony when Nick told him about Ronnie.

"Hey, that pretty waitress dropped something off for you just now. She told me to tell you to stick your charity up where the sun doesn't shine."

"Charity? I don't understand. What...oh, the money. I was pretty rotten to her and I felt bad, especially after what the cop told us. Why would she come to see you?"

"She thinks you're my lover. That you and I are gay lovers. Imagine that."

Devin bellowed so loud he made the boys cry. Nick took Anthony from Devin and hit him in the shoulder. Morgan was trying to sooth Markus.

"Why on earth would she think that? We were all together, so why did she pick me?"

"Actually, I think she thinks we all are, including Spence and Jamie. She didn't hang around for question and answer time, but she shoved your money at me to give to my lover. I hope you know this doesn't mean you get to sleep with Morgan. As my female lover, she is off limits to you," Nick told his brother as he sat his son back down.

"She say anything else? I mean, damn it, err sorry, Morgan, darn it, why would she think that?" Nick watched his brother play with Markus as he asked.

13

"I'm sure I don't know, but it matters very little now. Here's your money. You know you shouldn't carry around such a large amount of cash. You should let me...where do you suppose he's going?"

He gave up trying to get an answer from his wife as to why his brother took off without another word. She was off on another round of hysterics.

~*Chapter 3*~

It took Devin almost an hour to figure out which class Ronnie was in and another to figure out where the classes were being held. He had never realized that the Ohio State University campus was so huge. He had gotten lost twice on High Street and had driven around the stadium three times before he had figured out how to get off the winding road. It was nearly eight o'clock, by then and his mood had not improved.

Nick had been right about Devin not being mad about the gay part. He had several friends who had come out and several more who had not. One's sexual preferences had no bearing on his friendship with them. He just wanted to know why she had thought he was.

He thought about the information he had gotten at the bursars office when he'd stopped by to get her schedule. It seemed that the beautiful Ms. Frey needed to find herself another place to work out her internship or not be able to graduate on time. The lawyer that she had been working from had died suddenly over the past weekend and now she was in violation of her degree. An impressive one at that— Veronica Frey was very smart and would be sought after

15

from now until she graduated and signed with a firm. He had been right about her being close; she was in her last quarter.

Ronnie had a four point three six GPA and if that was not impressive enough, she also had a minor in Foreign Policy and Procedures and Corporate Law—two of Devin's specialties. When he found her, he was going to shake her hand then wring her pretty little neck.

Smiling, he thought touching the woman's neck first might be a better place to start.

At three o'clock in the morning, he found himself back at the diner again. He had had to drive around for nearly an hour trying to find it and now that he was here, he had no idea what he was going to say to her.

Devin had pretty much calmed down now. He was still pissed at her, but that was more because he could not find her than anything else.

He walked in the door just as she was coming out of the kitchen with another man. And Devin promptly got pissed all over again. Then when the man leaned over and kissed her—on the mouth no less—Devin saw red.

Both Devin and Ronnie watched as the man walked out the door and then she looked over at him. Devin was actually taken aback by the amount of venom he saw in her eyes. And more shocked at how quickly his cock hardened.

"What do you want? I'm really busy and, unless you are eating, then I suggest you get the hell out."

"I want to talk to you, please." Pulling her into his arms is what he really wanted to do, and kiss her until she could not breathe. But he figured that he valued his life and where all his manly parts were, thanks.

"Wrong. You eat something, you can stay. You speak and I'll call the cops on your ass. I suggest you go. I might actually spit in your food tonight."

They both knew she would not and he walked to the booth where her books were and sat down, picking up the menu.

He either had to sit down or fall down. All the blood in his body had pooled in his cock and he was suddenly dizzy with need for her. That made his mood all the more confusing. He'd only just met this woman the night before and she was doing all sorts of things to his libido.

Christ, she was beautiful, especially as mad as she was at him. Her strawberry blond hair was pulled back from her face showing high cheek bones, tiny ears and a long column of a neck. A neck he wanted desperately to lick and nibble. Her eyes were a bright polished purple color and nearly glowed with emotion. He already knew she was tall, but tonight she was a few inches taller in her black knee-high boots. The long expanse of leg in between those and her mid-thigh denim skirt was covered in dark tights. The sweater set she had on was a perfect contrast to her creamy skin tone, dark green undershirt, and a shade lighter outer shell. The set was tight and her hard nipples poked through deliciously.

Reaching under the table, Devin adjusted himself. It was either that or he was going to cause serious damage to his hard cock. He felt her come up behind him and hoped she was planning to pour the glass of ice water over his swollen member and not his head.

"I'll have the Manager's Special, eggs over easy and strawberries on the pancakes, please," he told her as he put the menu away and then looked up at her.

"Links or patties on your sausage? I also can do you some bacon, but it will take longer to cook up."

"Links. A cup of coffee and OJ as well." She had not bothered writing anything down, but he knew his order would be correct. He just was not sure if he would be eating it or wearing it.

He noticed the phone book open to the attorneys' section and pulled it and her neat notes toward him. There were several names on the sheet and all but three had been neatly crossed out. He also noticed that his name was not on the list and it had been crossed out of the phone book as well. Crossed out hard and with several lines going thought his name and a mustache on his face. Devin smiled at that. Apparently, she had figured out who he was. When she came back with his coffee and juice, he did not bother looking guilty.

"Do you understand the word privacy? As in stay out of others people's things when they don't concern you," she practically snarled at him.

"You left it out on my table—public domain. If it's out there, you must have wanted me to look at it." He thought she would argue that it had been her table first, but she simply started jamming her things into her backpack mumbling under her breath as she went. He wanted to laugh at her, but was afraid she would hit him with her Laws and Ethics book, which was about three inches thick.

A little while later, she brought him his platter of food and sat them before him. His eyes nearly bugged out at the sight. The pancakes were at least an inch thick and the eggs perfect, the yolks not even broken. Strawberries were sliced and in a bowl of heavy cream, and his sausages were golden brown and smelled like heaven. Everything was perfect.

When Devin ran his last bite of sausage through his yolk, he realized he had eaten the entire thing. He would need to run a few extra miles on the treadmill this week, but it had been worth every extra calorie he had put in his belly. He looked up when she brought the coffee pot again and to gather his plates.

"Everything was delicious. I don't think I've ever eaten anything so good in a very long time. I'd like to talk to you now, Ronnie."

"No." When she started to turn away, he stood up, taking the empty plates from her and setting them back on the table as he backed her up. The coffee pot was a little tricky, but he managed to get it from her without burning either of them. Still, he moved her backward. When she touched the wall with her back, he simply pinned her there with a hand to either side of her shoulders.

"I wanted to talk to you. I wanted to clear up that I'm not gay. Those other men you saw me with, they're my brothers. In fact, Spencer has a little girl and the man you met this morning at the office, Nicky, he has twin boys."

"Okay. Now that you told me, I want you to back up." Her voice was panicky, but also husky like his. When she stuck out her tongue to lick her lips, he thought he would die from need.

"No, not yet. Why did you assume we were gay, Ronnie? I just want to know. Not that it matters, but I'm curious what led you to that conclusion." He leaned closer to her, felt something poke him in the belly, and looked down at the gun she had in her hand. "Are you going to shoot me, Veronica? Because I would rather you didn't. At least not now. I'd really like to taste you first."

He leaned closer still and ran his tongue along the shell of her ear and then down to her lobe. Pulling it into his mouth, he nibbled gently on it as he moved his hand down her arm to her wrist. Suckling gently on the tasty morsel even as he moved her hand and the gun to her side, he stepped closer to her. Heat pulled at him from her and he wanted to taste her, any part of her he could wrap his mouth around. He pressed his erection into her soft folds and groaned.

"Do I feel like I'm a gay man to you now, Veronica?" Devin whispered in her ear. "Do you still think that I have a male lover when your body can do this to mine?"

He felt her stiffen and it took him several seconds before he realized that they were no longer alone in the restaurant and that she was talking to someone behind him. He pulled away from her ear, but not her body.

"...a point. He's done that. Now he's leaving."

Devin turned and saw the police officer from last night standing directly behind him in a stance that said, "I'll shoot your ass, no problem, if you don't move." Devin turned back to Ronnie in time for her fist to connect with is nose.

~~~

Ronnie might not have gotten into trouble if the stupid man had not hit his head on the way down to the floor and knocked himself unconscious. But she had hit him. Looking at her hand, she realized it burned and she felt stupid. Again.

Devin had only been trying to show her he was not gay. She had been so turned on that when he touched his body to hers she nearly came from his barely there touches. And the way he smelled. All sex and very male.

Then when he said those things about... She was not going to cry, at least not until she got home anyway. When the ambulance took him away, she went out to her car to go home.

Of course, her stupid car would not start and she had had to have Roger take her home. Tommy Bob, the restaurant manager and owner, had told her he would have to think about what to do about all this. He had never had any of his staff hit anyone before, not in all his fifty-six years, and he did not know what Mother was going to say about it.

"Ronnie, if that man presses charges, you could see jail time for assault. I'm not taking you to jail 'cause, frankly, I'm not sure what to do with you," Roger told her from the front seat of the cruiser as he drove. He would not let her sit in the front; she thought he was trying to make a point too. Damned men, why not just say what they meant? She wondered why they had to intimidate.

"I know, Roger. And you don't know how sorry I am about this. Thanks for not running me in."

She did not bother trying to explain why she had hit Devin Grant. What would be the point? She could hear the disappointment in his voice. Hell, she thought, she was disappointed in herself. She had never in all her life hit anyone before and she hated that she had done so now. And she didn't know what she would have done had Roger not shown up when he had. Devin was out cold and she had been trying to figure out how to revive him.

Ronnie was mad at herself because she didn't want to become her father. Her father hit. He had hit her with his fists or whatever was handy when she lived at home. One time he had beaten her badly with an orange race car track. She still had scars on the back of her legs and back from that. All her bones had been broken by him at one time or another, including her jaw five different times. And that all occurred in the first six years of her life. He was a mean son-of-a-bitch and she hated him with every breath she took.

Her mother, the drunken sot, had done nothing more than laugh when Ronnie had gone to her for help. Lindy had told her all men were pricks. It was just a matter of finding one that did not hit too hard or too often.

Ronnie had stayed away from men her whole life, avoiding them like they were carrying a disease that one could get by simply being next to them. She was more than likely the oldest living virgin at twenty-eight years old.

Going into the house after Roger had told her not to leave town until she heard from him or Grant's attorney — like she could — she went straight to her bedroom. Her hand hurt and she was sure that she was either going to lose her job or get written up. She could not afford to lose her job right now.

Ronnie's roommates were still asleep and she was very quiet when she walked by their room. Ben Kendal and Austin Pride owned the house and had been partners for nearly as long as she had been alive. Ronnie loved them dearly and was glad for their friendship. But right now she did not think she could deal with their drama. Smiling for the first time since this morning, she thought of the drama she would have to endure when she told them what had happened.

Filling up the huge tub in her bathroom with hot water and lots of bubbles, she stripped down and thought about the look on Devin's face when she had hit him. Looking at her hand again, she could already see the bruising start. Great, she thought, could this day get any worse? When there was a knock on her door, she seriously thought about sliding down under the water and staying there until she ran out of oxygen.

Opening the door slowly, Austin walked in. Without saying a word, he sat down on the toilet and played with the design embellished on his robe, only looking at her once in a while. Just when she was ready to scream at him, he spoke.

"Roger called. He said to tell you that you left your phone in his car and that Mr. Grant isn't going to press charges if you call his office first thing on Monday morning and do what he tells you to do. The number is by the phone in the kitchen. Then before I could find you, Thomas Bob called. He called to say he was sorry but he talked to his mother and they've decided that you must go. He said he's very sorry,

22

but his mommy still holds the money." Ronnie waited for more because she was sure there was. "That man is sixty-seven years old if he's a day. Why on earth he doesn't just put that old bat of his in a nursing home and grow some balls is beyond me. She probably doesn't even know she's driven him to seek men as a companion."

"I didn't know Tommy was gay. He seems so...straight to me whenever he comes into the restaurant."

Tommy was an odd sort of man. Given to fits of nervousness that made Ronnie think he was going to drop dead of a stroke at any minute. But he was nice to her and had let her work around her school. She didn't know what she was going to do now.

"I didn't say he was gay. I think he goes out with men because he is terrified of his mother. He probably thinks all women are like her and avoids them like you do men."

She did not comment on that. They both knew that was true. She did avoid men, all of them.

Austin dropped to the floor on his knees and picked up the plastic cup on the side of the tub and began pouring water over her hair. He had done this before, washed her hair when she was stressed and needed to talk. He did it so well she was nearly asleep when he spoke again.

"Do you wanna talk about it, love? You know I'll listen, and if you don't want Ben to know, well, we won't tell him. You know how old queers are, all drama and absolutely no help."

She knew he was trying to make her laugh and she also knew that he would tell Ben everything when he went back to bed with him. They were an awesome couple and so loving to each other and to her. She loved them both with all her heart.

"I'm becoming my father, Austin, and I don't want to," she told him quietly.

"Don't be stupid, girl. Your father is a crass prick who should have been put in prison years ago. Now tell me why you've come to this ridiculous conclusion. Does it have anything to do with this Grant person?"

Ronnie nearly laughed at the anger she heard in his voice. He may be the sweetest man she knew, but he was also not afraid to say what he thought.

"Yes. I hit him and knocked him to the floor. He was...he had...I thought he was gay and he had come to prove to me he wasn't. He made me mad and I hit him."

Austin did not say anything as he ran his fingers through her newly rinsed hair, working out the tangles. Then he let the long tresses hang outside of the tub to dry.

"I take it he proved it in a very manly way. Did he hurt you? No, I know he didn't. You would have shot him if he had tried that." He moved over to the toilet again and regarded her. "Ronnie, you know that Ben and I love you like our own child, but, honey, not all relationships are like mine and Ben's."

Ronnie burst out laughing as he had meant for her to do.

"Anyway. All men are not your father and most men never hit. You were just one of those unfortunate growing number of abused children and you have paid dearly."

Ronnie knew in her head he was right, but her heart thought differently. He handed her a towel and stood to leave.

"Ronnie, you have to give up this ridiculous notion of being him. You're human, honey, and you'll make mistakes. When you fall in love, and you will, it will be with someone who will love you despite who your family might be."

She sat up on her bed and laid her head on her knees after he had gone to bed and left her to sleep. She knew he was right. She knew plenty of men who did not hit first and then not ask questions at all. But she was still terrified because she had hit someone. She had hit someone hard enough to leave a mark. As she lay back, her head on her pillows, she felt the tears burn her eyes. Ronnie wanted so much to be normal, whatever that meant.

~*Chapter 4*~

"Grant Law Office. How may I direct your call, please?"

Taking a deep breath, Ronnie looked down at her notes and began reading them. She did better with notes than she did people. These notes she had worked on all week and over the weekend, and felt they were perfect.

"My name is Veronica Frey and I'm suppose to call—"

"Yes, Miss Frey. I've been expecting your call. Please hold while I transfer your call," the voice at the other end said.

"But I—damn it!" Hold music was all she was speaking to. "Damn it, damn it, damn it!" she said to the empty phone.

"Well, good morning to you too. Do you always cuss in the phone like that? If so, then we may have to work on your phone skills as well. What are you wearing?" Devin asked her quite suddenly.

She looked down at her jeans and t-shirt. "Excuse me?"

"What. Are. You. Wearing? I'm the one with the head injury, Veronica. You should be able to just look in the mirror and tell me what you have on."

Fine, she thought. "Blue jeans with a hole in the knee, a black Rocky Horror t-shirt that has seen better days, pink

27

KATHI S BARTON

underwear and a matching bra, and yellow socks and black boots. Satisfied? Now, why do you want to know?"

He was quiet for so long she had thought the call had been dropped. Then when he spoke, it was in that husky voice of his again. She felt a tingle down her spine and along her skin.

"Most women of my acquaintance would have told me that they were wearing a sexy negligee or nothing at all. But you tell me you're wearing underwear and not panties and I find that incredibly sexier. Christ, woman, the things you do to me."

"What the hell are you talking about? What do you care what I'm wearing? I have things to do today. I have a job to find and I have to figure out how to pay for school. I have an exam this week and I don't have time to sit around and talk to you about my underwear." His chuckle moved through her like a thunderstorm in the summer, fast and hot.

"You have twenty minutes to be at the downtown court house, circuit courtroom number three. Judge Tyler is the presiding judge. You had better be there, Veronica, or so help me, I'll have you arrested so fast your underwear will be the least of our problems."

Dropping the phone in the cradle, she sat there and stared at it. Then she jumped up and ran to her room. Twenty minutes did not give her a lot of time. She pulled out the only other nice outfit she had and threw it on. Pulling on her tights and boots, she was running out the door only to stop dead in her tracks. No car. Just as she was turning to run into the house and call the moron again, she saw Austin standing in the door with Ben. They were both grinning.

Austin tossed her his car keys. "We heard you running through the house like a herd of buffalo and thought you might need a car."

28

Running backwards away from them, she blew them a kiss and took off for the garage. She was going to be, late but she would arrive in style.

~~~

She was late. Five minutes so far. Devin was not sure she would actually show up, but he hoped so. Right now, he had to concentrate on his client and his case. His head pounded and his nose hurt every time he touched it. He had four stitches in his forehead and a black eye that was fading after five days. Damon had been pissed to be called to the hospital to take care of him, but had laughed for so long after finding out that a woman had hit Devin that he stopped bitching about it. Some days Devin really hated his family. They could be sarcastic pricks when the mood suited them. Which, he was coming to realize, was all the time.

Suddenly, there was a commotion at the back of the room and everyone turned to look at her.

Ronnie was blindly beautiful when she was angry, but looking at her all flushed with rushing, it was everything he could do not to go back and toss her against the nearest flat surface and fuck her until neither of them could walk.

Devin shook his head at that and tried to figure out why this one woman of all those he knew had affected him like she had. She had been in his mind all week at the oddest times. His date had ended early Friday night because he could not seem to concentrate on the woman he had been with at the time because visions of this one kept intruding in his mind. And his visions of her had not done her justice. The flesh and blood woman before him was truly amazing.

Devin nodded at his mother, who looked back at Ronnie. Margaret got up and went to get the younger woman and brought her to where his mother was holding a seat for them. There was a slight tussle that he knew that his mother would

KATHI S BARTON

win in the end about where they were sitting. It was not as if Margaret Parker was mean; he just knew that Ronnie's politeness would make her defer to the older woman. When Ronnie looked up at him, she was glaring so hard he felt it even after he turned back to the front of the courtroom.

"All rise, the honorable Judge James Tyler presiding."

"Your Honor, if it pleases the court, this is a total waste of the court's time and money. Mr. Carlos was caught with the stolen merchandise in his possession. My client denies any knowledge of the work of art and there is no proof that he had, in any way, any contact with the accused."

"If I had a dime for everyone who came through my court that said they were not guilty, I'd have retired twenty years ago. Now, sit down and shut up. Mr. Grant, this is a closed session. What, pray tell, is that young woman doing in here with your lovely mother?"

"I've brought her, Veronica Frey, to see if she could fit with my firm, sir. If it would please the court, I'd like to have Miss Frey second chair for me during these proceedings to see if we fit well together."

"Miss Frey, step up here, please," Judge Tyler said as he waved his hand at her.

"No. I mean, no sir, Your Honor. I don't want to work for him, or sit with him. I wasn't aware this was what he had in mind when he had me come here today or I wouldn't have come. He never gave me any details at the time I spoke to him."

"Miss Frey, I said to come up here. I don't like to be told no, especially in my own playground. Now!" Judge Tyler said to her, leaving no doubt she had better do as he said.

Devin had to smile, and he was working very hard not to laugh out loud when she poked him as she walked by. He had not had this much fun in the courtroom in ages. He

30

followed her one step behind. He may be having fun, but he was not stupid. Getting too close could give her easy access to his poor abused body.

"Miss Frey, didn't you work for Judge Simon? He was a good man and it was a hard loss to all of us. You must be at the end of you school, I'm thinking. You have someone else you're working for right now?"

"No, Your Honor. But I'm looking. I feel I have a lot of potential and, that being said, I should keep my options open. And not tie my horse, as it were, to a man I don't really care for." The judge looked taken aback for a second, but pressed on, his smile fighting hard not to turn into more.

"This man is offering you a good job right now. Any reason why you aren't falling on your knees thanking him for taking you on? You couldn't do much better than Devin Grant. He runs a respectable firm and he is well respected by his peers."

Devin heard her mumble something, but like the judge, had not heard it. He was sure it was not going to be flattering, but he was curious as well. Judge Tyler asked her to repeat it.

"I said I'd certainly like to try to find something better. Or at least someone with some manners. He is a rude, obnoxious man and I'd sooner work for a crook, Your Honor." Ronnie told the judge in a loud voice.

Devin's mother burst out laughing behind him and the prosecutor suddenly had a coughing fit. Judge Tyler glared at the man and winked at his mother. Devin thought that spanking the delectable Ms. Frey was becoming more and more promising.

"Miss Frey, are you aware you have on a sun dress in the middle of November? Isn't it a little chilly to be wearing such a...cooler weather dress? I realize that women of this day and age are always trying to make a fashion statement, but this seems a little extreme," Judge Tyler said mildly.

"I only have two dresses, Your Honor, and the other one is in the wash. It was either wear this, or my jeans and t-shirt." Devin closed his eyes and hoped she would not mention the pink bra and panties she had told him about earlier. She, thankfully, did not.

"Miss Frey, sit at the big boy table and hush up. I have a long court day and you might as well be a part of the fun too. And before you open that pretty little mouth and argue with me, I want you to know that it would be a very costly mistake to do so. Do I make myself clear?"

"Yes, Your Honor. Very clear. But I want it noted I don't like Mr. Grant very much. And I think he's an arrogant ass and needs to be stood in a corner for a decade or two."

"Duly noted, now sit down. First witness."

It was an hour into the trial when she suddenly sat up and looked at him. Devin had given her the file to look over while he waited for his turn now that the defense had rested. He saw her lean over to Mr. Carlos just as he stood to ask his questions of the witness, then she waved at him. Assuming that she wanted to speak to him, Devin went back to her to tell her now was not the time to start in on why she did not like him again. He leaned down to her after receiving permission from the judge to confer with his colleague.

"This list has been tampered with. See, after number ten, the type is different and there are smudges of some sort. Someone has removed something. Mr. Carlos said he had a thumb drive when he was arrested. And he doesn't know where it is."

Ronnie handed him the copy from his file. He could see the smudges she meant, and the typeface was smaller than the other information.

"What was on the thumb drive, Mark?" Devin asked his client. He did not know where this was going, but he would play along for a few minutes. His head hurt, but if he did not follow through on this, she would probably bop him on the head again.

"It was a recording of Mr. Peters selling me the painting. He didn't seem all that trustworthy to me so I had a camera set up of the whole thing. I didn't wanna be caught with my pants down. Beg pardon, ma'am." Devin looked at Ronnie, who blushed at the compliment.

"Well, that would have certainly helped your case. Who knew about this drive and when was the last time you saw it?" Ronnie asked him as she patted his arm. Devin didn't like that. He had no clue why, but he didn't want her touching anyone else but him.

"I gave it to the arresting officer and then I told that man over there I had it when he come to see me in jail." Mark pointed at the prosecutor. "He offered me a deal. If I was to take responsibility for the whole thing, then he'd see my kids went to college for free."

"Wouldn't it be great if you had that on tape as well?" Ronnie said, and Mark looked over at her and smiled.

"You did, didn't you? Why you sly devil. Too bad we don't know where it is. I don't suppose you made a copy of it, did you?"

Devin nearly shouted with joy when Mark nodded at her again. She had been sitting there for less than two hours and had solved a case he had all but given up on.

Devin looked at her as she smiled. It was not a friendly smile; actually, it was kind of scary. He was glad he was not on the receiving end of whatever she was thinking.

"I think Mr. Carlos should take the stand. I'm not sure, but I'm betting that that guy, Donaldson, knows where the drive is, don't you?"

Devin smiled and turned to the judge. He knew she was right too. Donaldson was the prosecuting attorney. "Your Honor, Miss Frey is going to call her first witness."

"No! Are you insane? Your Honor, he's insane, and you should have him put away. I can't call my —"

"Enough! Good Christ, you two fight like a married couple. Mr. Carlos, do you accept Miss Frey — and if you open your mouth, Miss Frey, I will slap you with a fine so fast your head will spin. Mr. Carlos, Miss Frey is going to take over your case. Are you all right with that?"

"Yes, sir. She is fine with me. She's a good girl."

"Mr. Grant, do you accept full responsibility for Miss Frey — quiet, girl, or I mean it — and her ability to conduct herself in a fair trial?"

Devin could see the steam rolling off her and wondered how she would hurt him when this was over. "Yes, Your Honor. I think she'll do a fine job."

"Good. Proceed."

~*Chapter 5*~

With her head between her knees, Ronnie tried to not pass out. Her head had started spinning the moment the judge had had the bailiff call the police and had the prosecutor, Donaldson, arrested. She was not sure of it all, just that he had stolen the drive that led to the arrest of his client, as well. Double whammy, Devin, err, Mr. Grant had called it. Now she just wanted to leave, and all she could do was concentrate on breathing in her nose and out her mouth and not the hand currently running up and down her back.

"Yes, she'll be fine. She skipped breakfast and this is her first win." Ronnie had heard this same line repeated half a dozen times since she had sat down abruptly and was not any happier about it now than the first time.

Devin was on his knees in front of her. She was sure his suit, now dusty from the floor, cost more than all the clothes she owned, and some of the other things she had as well. But she had to admit, the purple of his tie was really beautiful with the lavender shirt and gray suit. Then she remembered that she hated him.

"Will you stop telling people that? It is not my first win. I didn't win anything. He screwed up and got caught. How is that a win? He lost his job."

"In the event that you missed that in one of your classes, that's what you are going to be doing for a living. Finding a way to prove that people screwed up and catch them at it. How are you feeling?" He pressed her head down again when she started to say something — probably for the best since she was pretty sure it was not going to be all that nice. She stayed there.

When she looked up again, he was very close to her face. Very close. His breath felt warm on her cheeks and he smelled so good. Her mouth was simultaneously watering and dry and she wanted to press her mouth to his desperately.

When he started moving toward her, she licked her lips and felt her eyes flutter, wanting to close against the overwhelming feelings rushing her. His groan and quick flick of his tongue over her mouth had her reaching out to touch him — to pull him closer or to hang on, she was not sure. His cell phone chirping at that moment startled them both.

Pulling back slightly, he reached into his jacket pocket, pulled it out, and groaned again at whoever it was. Somehow, this groan did not do to her what his other had done.

"Let me call you back," he said into the phone and started to put it away, but stopped when the voice at the other end yelled.

"Wait, I have that information on that waitress. If you're smart, and I know you are, you'll avoid her like she's diseased. Her past is checkered and she has a family that makes Charles Manson look saintly. She's trouble, buddy."

Having heard the man at the other end, Ronnie pulled away from Devin and sat up. Her head was spinning, and she needed to get away. She stood up, moved to the table, and began to gather her things.

She had almost kissed the man.

Devin flushed and did not say anything for long moments. She was not sure if he was listening to more information or not because she could no longer hear the man at the other end.

"Yes. She's right here and, yes, I believe she heard you. Thanks." Another long pause and Devin hung up. He did not move from the floor, but regarded her from where he sat.

"I'm sorry you had to hear —"

"I have to go, Mr. Grant. I have a class this evening, and then I have to find…"

"Veronica, you work for me now. I'm sorry for what my brother Nicky said, but you can't have expected me to hire you without a background check and a thorough investigation. I have a reputation to maintain and a business to keep running."

"I didn't ask you to hire me. I never…I'm sure once you read the rest of his file on me, you'll change your mind anyway. I'm going…I have things to do. After reading my checkered past and my Mansonlike lifestyle, I'm sure there isn't a judge in the world who would hold you to the agreement you signed. Your secretary has my number if there is anything in there you can't understand."

She left the courtroom and was out on the front steps before she stared running. Ronnie could hear him yelling for her, but she did not know how much longer she could hold on to her tears and, if he caught her, she was done for. She was in the car and had it started before the floodgates opened and she started sobbing.

Ronnie had no idea how she made it home. Once she had gotten the car to start, the slot where the key went too blurry from her tears to get it the first time, she drove on automatic. Her family was all she could think of. Her family had fucked her again.

Ronnie had not seen most of them for years, probably ten or so. Her father would catch her off guard once in a while in the past and knock her around and take whatever money she had on her. She tended to avoid him and would hide if she saw any of them.

Thankfully, when she got to the house, both Ben and Austin were gone. The note on the table left for her said that they had gone to the store to get the things needed for Thanksgiving. She had forgotten about the holiday, which was in four days, and then she had the dinner thing on Saturday to go to with Austin as his "date."

Leaving a scribbled note to not wake her — she was really tired — she went to her room, stripped down, and climbed into bed. She thought she would toss and turn, but she laid her head down and went to sleep immediately.

The dream started where it always did. It was not really a dream, but a memory. When she had been younger, she had it nightly, waking up anyone that was near with her screams. That was how she had met Austin; he had heard her screaming one night while she hid behind a dumpster as he left the loft where he worked. He had taken her home with him and he and Ben had been her saviors since. She had been eight years old.

As she faded into the memory and her thoughts and feelings, her body tensed and she began fighting the blankets. She was on the floor near the door with her one blanket and no pillow as it usually was in this memory, just like she'd been so many nights all those years ago.

He was at them again, her father, the nasty bastard. And they loved it. Ronnie at six wished they would go to his bedroom to have the sex, and not right there in front of her or behind her, as was the case this night. Holly and Margo, her beautiful identical twin younger sisters, were their father's lovers. They were five. He had been "breaking them into the saddle" since the day they could satisfy him, which was nearly from the time they came home from the hospital at birth.

She knew as sure as she could breathe that it was sick and perverted. She tried telling someone about it once, but that had earned her a broken arm, six neat stitches in the back of her head, and a mighty headache to go with her troubles when her father had found out. She did not have to be told to shut up twice, thank you very much.

Holly was on the floor between his legs, and Margo was there as well, but to the side. He was panting and encouraging them, training them on the best way to pleasure him. She had her back to them, but she knew that they knew she was awake.

It would be over soon. Ronnie knew the signs, even if she never participated. Yelling out his completion, he looked over to his oldest child. With a slapped at Ronnie's shoulder to have her turn toward him, he said, "Tomorrow. Tomorrow, you are going to get broken in. I may have to put a bag over your ugly fucking head, but that will be my Christmas gift to you. So, be ready, or else."

Terrified, Ronnie remembered she could only stare at him. And continued to while Holly and Margo cleaned him up and he left the room.

Ronnie laid there for the rest of the night after her sisters had gone to their separate beds. Beyond shocked, she knew that at any moment he would make good on his promise and come for her. Even now she knew she never once closed her eyes that night as she waited in terror for him to come for her.

Her father always told her what he thought of her looks. She was nothing like the twins. Her hair was a dull, curly blonde, eyes purple like bruises, while they were blonde and blue eyed. Her father's perfect little girls. Oh God, what was she going to do? She had thought.

Christmas morning dawned beautifully. The sun came in through the kitchen window to find Ronnie standing on a stool making pancakes at the big ancient stove. They were fluffy and light, and crispy around the edges. She knew better than to make anything but perfect pancakes, or anything she had to cook for them for that matter. The rest of the family was in the living room, opening gifts around the big decorated tree, with the exception of her mother who was still in bed, drinking her Christmas away. Squeals of delight could be heard from the girls when they opened yet another gift.

Ronnie loved the music they played. But terror had kept a tight control of her enjoyment of the music. She had learned the hard way that if she showed any kind of enjoyment over anything, she would be denied it and hurt in the process.

Ronnie's enjoyment of anything had been a good source of pain and punishment from her father. He enjoyed hurting her any way he could and denying her something too…well, it was all the better, he'd told her often enough.

Once they were finished with their gifts, they came tromping into the kitchen to be served. And she did serve them too, carting food back and forth—drinks, syrup, and whatever else they needed. She would not be allowed to eat until her chores were done. But by then she was too exhausted to care to fix her anything so she usually ate a raw potato or a slice of bread to keep her from starving. Most nights she went to bed hungry more often than not, just too exhausted to do more than to strip down and collapse on her pallet on the floor.

As everyone was having their breakfast, Ronnie went into the living room to clear up the pretty papers and bows from their gifts. While finishing up, her father, Albert Frey, came into the living room to put his boots on. She was glad to see him going out; maybe he would forget about what he had said. She hoped that he would anyway.

He watched her for a few minutes, not saying a word to her. As he watched her, she tried to make herself as small as possible. He loved the terror he could see coming from her, and she had always been afraid of him. Small wonder the way he treated her. But this, this was a new terror of him, and he was enjoying it. She knew; she could see it in his eyes. His next statement made her realize that her hopes of him forgetting were all in vain.

"You remember what I told you? Last night, about you being broken in?" He barked it at her as a question.

"Yes, sir."

"Good. I'm going into town for an hour. When I get back, I'll get this over with, so I want you to be ready, hear me?"

"Why, sir? Why would you bother with me? I'm not good enough, nor pretty either." The moment the words left her mouth, she knew it had been a mistake.

He had backhanded her across the face so fast she had no time to brace for it and she ended up five feet from where she had been kneeling before the family tree. Pain ricocheted through her from the top of her head to the bottom of her feet. She made not a sound, for that would earn her another slap, harder than the first. She lay there feeling the blood trickle from her lip, not wiping it away no matter how badly she wanted to.

"You don't tell me what I'm gonna do, you hear me, bitch? I'm the man of this house. I make the decisions concerning all of you. You will do what I tell you when I tell you or else. You hear me?" The kick to her ribs was vicious and hard; air puffed through her lips and she felt the tears roll down her face.

"Yes, sir." She was whimpering now, not able to stop herself. More blood oozed from her nose and her lip and she was finding it difficult to breathe normally. She knew that this excited him, too, and tried to back as far away as she could from him.

He stood up, towering over her. He was a big man, at six-four and two hundred and twenty pounds, and his hands were like slabs of meat, big and hard. When he drew back his foot to kick her again, she heard Holly yell for him from the kitchen and he stopped.

"I'll be back in an hour," her father said between clenched teeth. "You will be ready, girl, or else. If I have to hunt you down, and make no mistake, because hunt you I will, I'll as soon kill you and be done with it. Hear me?"

"Yes, sir," she whimpered again.

He left. And as soon as the door closed behind him, Ronnie put plan "b" into action. She actually had a plan "a," but she knew that was a pipe dream, as she was only six, had no job, was not able to drive, and without any money, she would not get very far before he found her again and beat her worse for her troubles.

She hobbled up to her parents' room holding her side and trying not to get her blood on the wall as she held onto it to stay upright. She knew there would have been no chance of waking her mother up, not that she would do a damned thing about anything anyways. It was past noon, and the two six packs of beer that Ronnie had already taken up to her mother would have her feeling nothing by now. Pulling out the bottom drawer of the dresser in her parents' room, she pulled out what she needed and left again, not even trying to be quiet in the room.

Downstairs, Ronnie ushered her sisters to the new television and found them something they wanted to watch. She told them that she was going to clean the bathroom and she was using bleach. She knew that they would not have come in there for anything. They did not want to ruin their pretty clothes. Neither of them mentioned the blood on Ronnie's face, nor did they act as if they cared, which Ronnie knew they didn't.

Knowing that her time was very limited, Ronnie went to the half bath, spreading clean towels around the floor. Taking off her bloodied shirt and pants, she folded them neatly and set them aside on the toilet seat. Standing in her panties and semi-clean t-shirt, she pulled out the thirty-eight special she had gotten from her parents' bottom drawer. She knew how to use it, as she had looked it up in the library, and made sure that there was at least one bullet in the chamber. It was almost too heavy for her little hand, but she was desperate. Then, without another single thought, she pointed the pistol to her temple and pulled the trigger.

There was a bump to her shoulder, and a searing pain in her head. These two things registered instantaneous. Pain was not anything she had expected. She had thought that, as a dead person, she would be, well, dead and without pain. She also felt her forehead hit the small sink on her way to the floor. There had been a smile on her face; she knew this. She had felt at peace for the first time in her very young life. Peace and happiness at leaving behind the world that had done all that it could to make life so miserable for her short time on this earth.

Ronnie had woken up screaming—at least in her head—in the hospital room. She had not been able to do anything very well with her face wired together, but she did try to look around. The pain shot through her like a rocket. And then, just as suddenly, she was down again, slipping into the welcoming darkness. Over the next few weeks, that was how her life was measured, horrible pain then thankful darkness with only a few minutes of awareness with each awaking.

After two months of drifting in and out, Ronnie opened her eyes fully one morning. She had been waking more and more, but had made sure of who was in the room with her before she made her wakefulness known to others. She could stay conscious more and more during the day, though she hid that as much as she could too. She still had pain, horrible, gut-wrenching pain, but she was getting better at seeing past it. At times, when she saw her father there, she simply did not move and waited for him to leave again. He rarely stayed long anyway and would only sit and watch the television in the room, ignoring everything but it.

She looked around the room she was in, trying to find an escape route, even though she could not move. That was when she saw the woman policeman. Why, oh, why? *How could someone be so cruel?* she thought when she realized she was still alive.

"Hi, honey. How are you doing? I know you can't talk very well, but can you blink for me? Blink once for yes, two times for no." The officer moved in front of Ronnie. "I'm here to keep you safe, to protect you, you understand? I want you to trust me to keep you safe. They never caught the man who did this to you and we don't know if you saw him or not. We don't want to take the chance of him coming back. Can you remember what happened?"

Someone had been asking her those same questions every time she woke up for the past few days. She wanted to scream that yes, she had seen the person who hurt her, but no, she did not know how she came to still be alive. She had gathered from the talk around her that the story was someone had broken into her family's home and tried to rob them while her parents were out spreading Christmas cheer in the neighborhood. And Ronnie, God bless her stupid little tough soul, had taken it upon herself to save her terrified little sisters from all manner of harm. For her troubles, Ronnie had gotten herself beaten to a bloody pulp and nearly killed. But she had saved the day, her sisters and Christmas, thank the Good Lord. If she could have, she was sure she would have puked.

Ronnie just stared at the policewoman. Trust? Who was this woman kidding? Trust? No, was not anything she would ever give again.

"My name is Officer Frey, Mary Frey. I want to help you. All right?"

Ronnie may have been only six, but she was far from stupid. She did not blink at the officer, but had turned away and closed her eyes. She knew there was no help for her, not from this person, or anyone else. So, as she had every other time, she pretended to slip into the abyss of welcoming darkness and escapism.

Six months later, she was gone. Planning, hording foodstuffs, and pretending got her away.

~*Chapter 6*~

Ronnie woke with a start and looked over at the clock beside her bed and realized that it was only one o'clock in the morning. She got out of bed and took a shower. She knew from experience that she would not get any more sleep tonight. After leaving her bedroom, she made her way to the kitchen.

Ronnie baked when she was depressed. She baked cookies mostly, though sometimes, she would whip up a batch of cinnamon rolls or a cake or two. Ben always made sure there was at least two twenty-five pound bags of flour in the pantry and enough sweet add-ins that bakeries would be in awe. She pulled out the big bag and took it to the kitchen to work off some stress.

Ronnie did not need recipes to cook. She had been cooking since she was old enough to pull a chair over to the stove on her own. And she could dream up more concoctions that turned out perfectly than Ben could cook with step by step instructions. When Ben came into the kitchen later that morning, she looked up in surprise. She thought she had woken him up.

"I could smell the sweetness all the way upstairs. Is there anything for breakfast yet, or do I have to wait?" he asked her with a huge grin.

Ronnie looked up at the clock over the stove and was startled by the hour. Ronnie looked around the room as if seeing it for the first time. She had been baking for nearly six hours and the room looked it.

There were cookies cooling on every flat surface of the room and some surfaces that were not. There were also trays and trays of stacked cookies, all decorated and iced. Peanut butter ones with white and dark chocolate drizzled on the top. Small sugar cookies decorated and dressed with sprinkles and hard frosting. No bakes had firmed up and were now ready for the containers, and tiny pecan tarts were golden brown and still warm from the oven. There was a batch of fresh cinnamon rolls topped with browned pecans rising in two pans near the warm oven, waiting to be baked for a breakfast treat. Coffee that turned on automatically dinged when she looked at it. It had just finished brewing.

"Oh, Ben, I'm so sorry. I'll pay for all this. Maybe we can give them away for gifts or something. I was just going to bake a few then try and go back to bed. I'm so sorry." She was crying and could not seem to be able to stop. Even with all the baking, her level of stress was very high.

"Oh, darling, don't cry. You know we don't want you to pay for this. Our employees enjoy the hell out of all this. I'll go down to that container store today and pick up some really nice Christmassy sealable ones and you and I will divide them up into gifts. How many you think we'll need? Five...maybe six hundred?"

When she started to cry and laugh, Ben pulled her into his arms and held her. She loved these men. They were the best in the world. And she wanted to stay in Ben's arms forever. The phone ringing did not stop them from their humor and Ben answered it full of silliness.

"Ronnie's house of ill repute and baked goods, the place where, if you want it hot and naughty, then we have it for you. Head food taster Ben speaking."

She watched as he closed his eyes for a brief second then looked over at her and shook his head. Ronnie knew it was Mr. Grant even without him telling her so and started shaking her head as well.

"Yes, she's here, but I'm not so sure she wants to talk to you right now. Why don't you call back in a few years, preferably in about thirty? I can do that, but I guess you'll need to ask that one yourself. Hang on." He turned and put the phone on hold and looked at her. "He has some questions about your family and he said that you told him to call if he needed answers. How did he get that information, Ronnie?"

"He had his brother do a background check on me. But it was bound to come out sooner or later. I'm actually surprised that someone hadn't mentioned it before now. Is he mad?"

"He doesn't sound like it, but I could be wrong. Do you want to talk to him? If not, you know I can take care of this for you."

And he would, too, she knew. But she had told Devin to contact her if he had questions. She just wondered if he would think of her differently, but then realized that he already did. She reached for the phone and pushed the hold button to talk.

"Mr. Grant. It's Ronnie Frey. What can I do for you?"

"My name is Devin, Veronica. I have a few questions I'd like answered, if you have time. I'd really like to do this face to face instead of over the phone. Can you come by my office today? I have time this morning until eleven, then after three the rest of the day."

"I have a test at ten and it runs until six tonight. I can leave after I'm finished, but I don't know how long it will be. My Tuesday and Wednesday class is from nine until eleven, Mr. Grant. I think classes will be canceled for Friday, but I don't know what the profs will do."

"I want you to call me Devin. All right, I'll see you here after your test today. Veronica, I'll expect you to be honest with me on this. I have your complete file and there are things I'd like to talk to you about before we begin our working relationship."

"I'm always honest, unlike some people. I'll come straight there after class, Mr. Grant." And she hung up on him and whatever he had been saying.

~~~

He was laughing when he hung up. She was such a contradiction at times. One minute, the hard nosed woman who could take on the world, the next, a girl who would call him "Mr. Grant" because she knew it would irritate him.

He looked down at the file again and the pictures spread out over his desk, and sobered. It was hard for him to equate the woman he knew now with the child in the photos. Picking up one particularly horrific one, he tried to see her face in the shot.

She looked broken. And the amount of blood was staggering. The doctor's report meant nothing to him, but he read it anyway. She had had nearly every bone in her body broken and some more than once. The report said that she had been found in the back yard of the family home in a pit of some sort. It was believed that the person who had tried to rob the house when the adults had been away had taken her with him. Ronnie was not found until three days later by the neighbor's dog sniffing around in the yard. She had been near death and had it not been for the extreme cold temperatures, she would have been.

Devin called his brother Damon and asked him to come down as soon as he could. Damon was in his office on the second floor of the Grant building and Devin remembered Damon telling him over the weekend that he was only going in this week to finish up some paper work and have the decorators come in and decorate the office for Christmas. He told Devin he would be down in ten minutes.

"I had Nicky start an investigation on the girl that I have working for me. Veronica Frey. She has a closed file in her records that came to me this morning that no one but you and I know about. I want you to read this report and tell me if it's as bad as I think it is." He handed the thick file to his brother as Damon sat down.

"Am I doing something illegal, Devin?" Damon asked even as he opened up the file and began reading.

"No, it is a closed file, but she gave me permission to look into her past when she signed off on me doing a complete background check on her. She's coming in later to answer some other things I have questions about. But this file...this one scares me, Damon. I'm hoping it's not near as bad as I think it is."

While Damon read the report, Devin kept himself busy with emails and phone calls. It seemed the legal system did not take holidays. It was perhaps an hour later when Damon threw the file back on his desk.

"This girl, the one in the pictures and the file, it's your waitress, isn't it?" Devin did not bother correcting him about it being his waitress, but nodded that he was right. He wanted her to be his waitress and a whole lot more, but right now, he was not sure where they stood. He did, however, want this repost to be better than he thought it was. But he was pretty sure it was going to be worse. Much, much worse.

"Yes. She works for me now, as an intern. She'll graduate at the end of this quarter, in January." He let his brother go at his own pace.

Damon was a processor and Devin knew that he had thrown a lot at him. He watched as Damon paced back and forth. He knew that his brother was a great doctor and something like this, child abuse at this level, would take some time to process.

"The medical records show a six-year-old little girl with enough wounds and injuries that would kill most kids, yet she is still alive. I doubt there is a bone in her body that had not been broken either by what those pictures show or prior to that. According to the records, she spent several months in physical therapy before she disappeared from the hospital one day. What do the records say happened to her and what caused that trauma to her body?"

"That she took on an intruder that was bent on robbing the house and harming her family. She single-handedly kept him from hurting her little sisters who were almost five at the time."

"You don't believe that any more than I do. Did you notice the reference to a single gunshot wound to the head? There was also gun residue on her left hand. What does it say about that?"

"They have no idea, but they guess that she tried to shoot him and he shot back. Damon, what are you thinking?"

Devin hoped they were not on the same path, but he knew that his brother was thinking the same thing when he turned to look at him. Christ, that poor little girl.

"I believe she shot herself. Christ, Devin, she was six fucking years old, the same age as Meggie. I can't imagine what could drive a child to feel the need to take such drastic measures that she would put a gun to her head and pull the trigger, could you? Was there no help for her? What about her family. Where were they during this time?"

"According to the report, they were out spreading Christmas cheer to the underprivileged. They returned to their home to find the front door broken in and Veronica gone. The little girls were safe and hiding in an upstairs closet where Veronica had told them to hide."

"They left those children there alone! Christ! Spencer won't even go to the mail box without finding a sitter for Meggie. I don't believe that any more than I do the gun shot. Fucking bastard hurt her, didn't he?"

Devin could not say for sure, but he had a pretty good idea that he had. Devin had never seen a case like this before. But knowing what he had found out about her family from the file Nicky had called him about, he thought the father had had a lot more to do with this than he had said.

"Damon, I like this girl. I like her a lot. She has something about her that draws me in. I'm not sure...she irritates me to the point where I want to strangle her, and other times to the point I want to..." He wanted her, but he could not tell his brother that, even though he was sure he got it.

"Is it because she is so different, or is it because she repels you so much?" Damon was laughing at him.

Devin bristled. Veronica did not repel him, not really. She was mad at him and he felt he deserved that, but repel? Nah, he would grow on her.

54

~*Chapter 7*~

"Grant Law Offices, how may —"

"It's Ronnie Frey, please don't transfer me or put me on hold, Mrs. Justice. I don't have enough money to buy any more minutes on this blood sucking machine, and I have to get back to class very soon. All right?"

"Yes, Miss Frey. What can I do for you?"

"There is a family emergency at home so no one can pick me up after class to take me to his dickship. I have to take the bus and the bus system is a lot to be desired this time of year. If Mr. Grant isn't there when I get there, then I'll go home — and just between us, I hope he's not. I've had a really shitty day. Otherwise, I have no idea when I'll be done here and there. Shit, what a mess. Sorry. Okay?"

"Yes, Miss Frey. I'll let Mr. Grant know. Is there anything I can do for your family?"

"No, I've —" The phone when dead.

~~~

There was a knock at his door and Devin looked up from the file he was supposed to be working on. He told Caroline Justice to come in. He was not getting anywhere anyway. For the past ten minutes he had been staring at it without seeing it. All he could think about was the woman whose file was in the bottom of the drawer of his desk. What she might say to him when she came tonight.

"Mr. Grant, Miss Frey just called. She's having a bit of a problem with transportation."

He looked down at his phone, saw that no one was on hold, and closed his eyes. He just knew whatever the message was, he was not going to like it.

"What trouble has she managed to get herself into now?"

"She called to say there is an emergency at home and that she will be running behind a bit. Her ride will not be able to pick her up. She will be taking the bus and believes that the unreliability of the system will make it so that she will not be on time for your appointment with her."

"Call the little twit back and tell her that I'll come and get her. What happened to her car anyway?"

"I'm not sure, sir. She didn't say. She seemed quite upset. The reason I couldn't transfer her to you is she was out of money."

Devin gathered up is jacket and coat. He was all the way to the door when he realized what she said. He turned back.

"Out of money? What does that have to do with transferring the call?" Devin could feel a headache coming on.

"She called from a payphone, I believe. She called it a bloodsucking machine and that it would cost her more if I did."

Devin left. It took him forty minutes to get to the university, and he was sitting out front of her building when she came out. He still had her schedule and since that night driving around to find her, he had a better understanding of the campus area.

Her smile took his breath away. Starting the car to warm it back up for her, he got out and walked to her. She did not see him at first, but when she did, he saw the smile crumble to be replaced with a frown and then anger. He had to smile. This woman was as unpredictable as Ohio weather.

"Come on and get in. The car's toasty and warm. I've made us reservations for dinner and we'll go there before we go back to the office and talk."

"No. I have a pass and I'll take the bus. You go get your dinner and I'll meet you at the office as soon as I can." She started to turn away when he grabbed her arm.

The sidewalk was slick and she started to tumble. Rolling her into his arms as he fell with her, he took the impact as his back hit the ground and she landed on top of him. With the wind knocked out of him, he held her to him as he struggled to breathe. Her body moving over his was not helping him at all.

"Stop moving," he shouted.

She stopped immediately. But that opened up a whole other issue. She was on top of him, all of her pressed completely over him. Heat surged through him, need hurled through his body, and his cock hardened. Thinking a change of position might help, he rolled her off him and onto her back. Now she was beneath him.

"Veronica, this isn't... Christ, you are very beautiful, aren't you?" Lowering his head slowly, he could not help but think that he was going to taste her, finally.

Before he touched his mouth to hers, her tongue darted out and ran across her lips, wetting them. He groaned and licked the wetness, tasting her. Moaning, he crushed his mouth over hers.

Mine. All he could think about as soon as he touched her was that she was his. Moving his hand to her hair, he pulled her closer and slid his tongue along her lips, and nearly whimpered when she returned the favor. When her hand curled around his neck, he slid his leg over hers and rocked into her. He needed her, now. The pain in his hip jerked him back. Someone had just kicked him.

"Hey, buddy. I want you to gets off Ronnie. The ground is cold and she might get a cold where she can't take cough medicine. My momma says that to me all the time. Hey, Ronnie, you okay? He hurting you?"

She nearly unmanned him in her hurry to get up. He wanted to lay there and gather himself. But the man was right and this was a public place and he wanted to most definitely take it somewhere where she was not in any danger of getting a cold. He slowly got to his feet, hoping his erection would calm down before he had to turn to face either of them.

"I'm fine. I fell and he caught me. I...I have to go. Thanks for...I'll see you back at your office. I have to go...I think that...I have to go."

Devin was caught off guard by how flustered she was. Innocence mixed with her swollen lips from his kisses and erect nipples that pressed again her sweater had him groan again.

"Ronnie, get in the car, please. There is no reason for you to ride the bus when I have a perfectly good car right over there."

"She don't gotta ride with you, mister. She's a big girl, and if'n she don't wanna ride with you, then you ain't gonna make her. Ronnie, you go on and catch the bus, okay? I'll stay here and teach this fancy man that women don't gotta do what he says. I won't hurt him too much."

Devin looked at her and wondered if she would leave him there. They both knew that this man planned to try and beat a few lessons into him. She stood there and chewed on her lower lip and looked between the two of them.

"I'll go with him, Billy. He's my...I have to answer some questions and I might as well go with him to get it over with. Thanks, though. You're a good man." She patted the older man on the back and smiled that dazzling smile at him. She had never looked at him like that and he tried not to be jealous of the obvious affection she had for this older man.

Devin reached out for her hand and waited. He could see the anger on her face and also her indecision. He could wait as long as it took, he thought. When she finally reached out and laced her fingers into his, he wanted to jump for joy. But all he did was take her backpack from her shoulder and lead her to the car. After settling her inside, he looked over at the man who had kicked him.

"Thank you, Billy. It's good to know that Ronnie has a protector here, someone to keep an eye out for her. I know that I'll rest easier knowing that you're around."

"You her boyfriend? If'n you are, you should know that that man has been back looking around. He don't look to me like he means to be nice to her. Want I should call the police when I sees him again?"

Devin looked at the woman in the car and back at Billy. Reaching into his pocket, he pulled out his card and walked back over to him.

"You call the police then call me. My phone number is on the front and my cell number I'll put on the back. ou have a cell phone, Billy?" Billy nodded. "Good, call me when he comes around again. I don't care when it is, please call me."

"Yeah, I can do that. He's a mean man. I can tell. Mean men like him hurt girls. I don't hurt nobody. That's why the college lets me clean the floors and take out the trash. I gots a good job and I like Ronnie; she's good to me. Always nice to me and never makes fun of me. She gived me some mittens last time it got cold. I like Ronnie."

"I like her too. Thanks again. And, Billy, sometimes women don't like it when men think they need protecting, so I think we should keep this just between us men. What do you say?" He put out his hand to the older man and hoped he would not be putting him in a position that would get him hurt or in trouble.

"Yeah, my momma said that. She said that girls are strange and that I should just agree with them and walk away. She told me it was safer. Ronnie, she is nice. I like her."

As their hands clasped, he heard the door to a car open and turned to see Veronica step out. When Billy waved at her, she waved back and stepped back into the car.

Going back to his car, Devin wondered who Billy had seen and hoped it was just the overactive imagination of an overprotective man. But he did not think so. He was afraid that Veronica's father was hanging around.

~~~

She sat in the warmth of his car and wondered what the hell Devin could be talking to Billy about. Ronnie knew that he would not hurt Billy, he was too much of a gentleman to do that, but they seemed to be getting very chummy. She was about to get out of the car again and see what they were doing when she saw Devin coming toward her.

He had kissed her. She had kissed him too. Running her fingers over her lips, she could swear she could still feel the warmth from his mouth. She had felt his hardness against her when he shifted over her; his cock moved along her belly and she felt her body respond to him. Never had she felt the...emotions, needs, wants—all that and more—when a man had kissed her and his body touched her like Devin had.

When he finally got into the car and looked at her, her face flushed when she remembered how she had pulled him closer and surged against him. She wondered how much further they would have gone if Billy had not come along and brought them back to earth.

"What are you thinking? Tell me what is going through your mind right now," Devin asked her in his gently demanding voice.

"We shouldn't have done that. I work for you and we shouldn't have done that." She blurted it out before she could hold it back and then felt her face heat more.

"You're right; we shouldn't have done that right there. But that doesn't mean that I don't want to do it again and that I don't want to go further. I won't lie to you, Veronica. I want you. I want you very badly. I want to taste you, surge inside of you deep. I want to make love to you in the worst way."

"I...I work for you, Mr. Grant. I..."

"Veronica, if you call me Mr. Grant again, I'm going to bend you over my knee and spank you. Not that that doesn't have its own appeal, but we'll work up to that. For now, my name is Devin. Devin Grant. Say it, please?"

"Why? What could you possibly want from me that thousands of other women, women more in your league, couldn't give you? Is it just the sex? That couldn't be it. I'm neither sexy nor beautiful. I'm not terribly smart, I don't have any money, and I—"

His mouth was suddenly over hers. Sliding closer out from under the steering wheel, he put his hands at her waist and pulled her into his lap, never breaking his mouth from hers. Moving her and adjusting her body, she was soon straddling his lap, her legs on either side of him. As he cupped her ass and pulled her forward closer to his body, his mouth moved down her throat and over her collar bone. Her body was on fire, lava replaced her blood, and her breathing had become ragged.

When his hands, hot and hard, spread across her bared ribs and pulled her forward, she moaned, grabbed his shoulders and threw back her head. His cock was pressed hard into her, and he rode her over him, moving her up and down his hardness with his hands gripping her tight. His mouth, seeking, found her breast, he bit through her clothes and into her nipple as she came apart, screaming through her first release.

There was not a part of her that she thought had been deprived of her release. Even her nipples ached and felt tender. Her heart pounded hard in her chest and she felt dizzy with it. Leaning forward, she laid her head onto his shoulder when she could claim her body again. As the tremors slowed and her heart was not pounding like a jack hammer, she started to stiffen and she could feel the tears start to well in her eyes.

"Don't, love. Just let me hold you for a minute longer," he crooned to her as he stroked her back and held her in his arms.

What had she done? she thought. She waited for him to...to what? Pulling back, Ronnie looked at him. His eyes were dark and she could see his need within them. The pulse at his throat pounded like hers had and she found herself wanting to take it into her mouth and nip at it.

"You didn't come. You didn't get your...you weren't satisfied. Are you going to hurt me now?" She hated the sound of her voice, the sound of a small child.

"No, never. I will never hurt you, I promise." He moved her hair from her eyes and continued to stare at her.

She did not know why, but she believed him. She laid her head back on his shoulder and stayed that way for several minutes before he pulled her back and looked at her.

"How about we go to dinner then I take you home?" He brushed her hair from her face again and moved her to the seat, buckling her into the seatbelt. She did not know why, but she felt strangely happy about his concern.

"I would rather just go home. Please?" He moved back under the wheel and put it into gear. He did not look at her; she knew because she was staring at him.

"All right."

Other than her giving him her address, neither of them said anything on the drive to her house. She did not say anything when the car stopped, but opened the door and ran to the house before he had the key turned off. She was inside with the door shut when she heard him walking up the stairs to the porch. Ronnie stood there with her back to the door and waited for him to knock, to demand to finish what they had started in his car. But he did nothing, and soon she heard the car start again and. When she looked out, he was gone.

~*Chapter 8*~

Ronnie was watching television with Austin when the phone rang later that night. She thought it was probably Ben. She began picking up their empty popcorn bowls to take them to the kitchen.

Ben had had to stay overnight at the hospital because they were concerned about the large bump on his head. When he had slipped on the ice at the market, he had hit his head on the parking sign. Austin answered the phone, and then handed it over to her with a grimace.

"Hello?" She had no idea who it could be; it was nearly ten o'clock and everyone she knew was here or at the hospital.

"Who was that who answered the phone? Why the hell do you have someone there this late?" The voice was snarled and angry and she was not sure who it was at first.

"Mr. Grant?" His growl made her nipples harden.

"It's Devin, damn it. And you didn't answer my question. Why is there a man there with you at ten o'clock at night?"

"It's his house." She did not understand his wanting to know at first, and she was not happy with his tone either. What right did he have to question how she lived her life?

"You live with a man." It was not a question, but she answered anyway.

She looked over at Austin, who was shaking his head at her. When she raised a brow in question, he sliced his finger across his neck. She wondered if he wanted her to hang up or shut up.

"Yes, two of them, as a matter of fact. Again, what business is it of—"

"The reason I'm making it my business is because I nearly had sex with you today. I had your nipple in my mouth and you came all over me. Were you planning to tell me, or them for that matter? What sort of person are you? Or do they already—"

As his voice grew with each word, so did her temper. She had learned to keep a tight rein on her redhead temper, but he had pushed her buttons just one time too many over the past few days.

"Listen here, you arrogant son of a bitch. I did not ask for you to come get me today, nor did I offer my nipple or any other part of my anatomy to you. I wanted to take the fucking bus, and, in fact, insisted on it. But oh no, the high and mighty Devin Grant had to have his way, because to you I'm too stupid to know what I want. Well fuck you! I will work for you until I have my results back and when they come in, I'm going to be out of there so fast it'll make your pretty head spin, you maniacal, chauvinistic asshole. Do not call me again, do you hear me?" She pushed the end button on the phone and screamed. Her body was pulsing with anger and she felt her heart pounding with it.

"Throw it."

Austin startled her; she had completely forgotten he was there. She looked at his grinning face.

"I find cordless phones to be a major frustration too when you can't slam it down in the cradle when you hang up. I miss those days. So I just throw it at the wall—just don't hit the television. Ben will be pissy enough as it is without taking his soaps away from him. Throw it, Ronnie. I'll replace it."

And she did just that. It hit the far wall with a resounding crash. Pieces of the receiver flew everywhere and a small dent in the wall board had a long piece of wire embedded into it. Looking at the mess she had made and the dent in the wall, Ronnie sat down on the couch and burst into tears.

"I hate that man. He did everything but call me a slut, Austin. I've never even been with a man and he is the first...the first one that I...oh, Austin." Sobs tore from her throat and her heart.

"Want me to beat him up for you? Or could I have a few of our friends make a pass at him? Hum, I think I like that one. Let me do it, please?"

In the end she, would not let Austin do anything to Devin, even as much as she wanted to herself. He had hurt her. More than she had thought possible. Her entire life she had avoided men and the one time she found herself wanting go get close to one, he turned out to be a prick.

On Wednesday morning, Ronnie was at the Grant building early. Mrs. Justice took Ronnie around and showed her were everything was and then led her to a room so that she could work in quiet.

The room was beautiful and Ronnie fell in love with the huge desk that took up most of the room. It sat in front of the window that looked over the skating rink below. The desk was made of a light walnut and the drawer pulls were brass-colored. The antiqued-looking green lamp in the center looked regal and warm.

There were several files on the corner closest to the door and a large box filled with office supplies — pens, folders, a stapler, and other items that one would need to work.

On two of the walls were wall to ceiling book shelves filled with beautiful law books. Most of them look to Ronnie as if the binding had never been broken; others looked well loved and used. Some of the shelves had small items, a framed picture, and a couple of ceramic pieces. A few of those she recognized as a favorite artist of Austin's. The third was the window and it was massive in its size and view. Looking down there was the rink, but out the vista was expansive as well as beautiful. Ronnie imagined, in the spring, the view would be spectacular. The fourth wall was blank other than the door they were standing in and another one that was closed just down from them near the corner.

"Mr. Grant called and said to have you look over these files there on the desk. He said that if you need anything just to let me know and I'll make sure you have it. There is a computer being set up in here later this afternoon and a printer will be delivered tomorrow. Your extension is four. Oh, I'm supposed to ask you what your cell phone number is and to make sure you have Mr. Grant's. Is there anything else that I can answer for you now, Ms. Frey?"

"No, I'm fine. I don't have a cell phone. I need to leave at eleven today; I have a class. He knows that, right?" She was not going to ask where he was just as long as he was not around. She really didn't care.

"He is aware of your schedule, I believe. I'm not sure about the cell. I've actually never known anyone...it doesn't matter. I'll be here until you leave. The office will be closed on Thanksgiving and Friday after for the holiday. If there is anything you can think of, just jot it down and I'll take care of it for you."

"Thanks, Mrs. Justice. I'm fine."

Ronnie moved to the desk, picked up the first file, and started reading. It was not long before she was making notes in her steno pad and pulling down books.

At ten forty-five, Ms. Justice knocked on the office door and called out for Ronnie. She was on the floor behind the desk. She popped her head up and grinned at the older woman.

"Ms. Frey?"

Ronnie sat down on her knees and started pulling the large tomes into a pile to be returned to the shelf. "I'm coming. Thanks for reminding me. I get caught up sometimes in what I'm doing. I should bring in the timer I use at home." Ronnie finished putting the books away and gathered up her things for class.

Picking up two of the files on the desk, she handed them to the older woman. Ronnie had left sticky notes on the folders and copious notes on the inside. She knew they were thorough, but did not know what Mr. Grant would think about her work. And she was reasonably sure she didn't care either.

"These two are complete. I put all the references on the front for him. I tried not to scribble so that you could read my notes, but sometimes my mind gets ahead of my fingers. The more obscure references, I marked the page, paragraph and line for you as well. I'll finish the other two and whatever else he needs done on Monday. That is, if it's okay. If not, then would you mind leaving me a detailed list of things he does want and does not?"

"Of course, my dear. But I'm sure these will be fine. And your handwriting is very neat and readable. You hurry now or you'll miss your class."

Dragging her coat behind her, Ronnie moved out of the office and to the stairwell quickly. Taking the stairs for the exercise, she ran down them as quickly as she could. By the time she burst out of the front of the building, the bus to take her to the university was just pulling up.

Glancing around, she thought she saw Devin, but turned back and stepped into the bus. Sitting down, she did not look up again until the bus was a good three blocks from the building. Settling down in the seat, she closed her eyes against the glare off the snow and thought about her class today. She loved her classes and was slightly nervous about finishing up so soon.

Class had let out early and she returned home exhausted and sore. She had not slept well the night before and the dream had returned, making sleep impossible after she woke. This time, she had screamed awake and had awakened Austin too. She felt bad about that all day.

Going into the kitchen for a much needed glass of iced tea, she found a box with her name on it and an envelope. A note from Ben said that it had been delivered for her at around one o'clock. Deciding to read the message in the envelope first, she sat down and opened it.

"Unlimited everything so don't be afraid to use whatever you need. It's already been programmed with the following numbers. Let me know if you have any problems. Devin."

There was a list of names and the corresponding key to push to call them. Devin's was first, of course. She just glanced at the other names, none of which she really knew. She didn't even try to guess why he would feel she needed Margaret Parker's name.

She opened the package next and a state of the art cell phone slipped out and into her palm. Without even playing

70

around with it, she stuck it into her jeans pocket and cleaned up the mess she had made on the table.

Ronnie knew she would never use the phone for anything other than answering his calls. So what did she care how the camera worked or it the ring tones were set up? As far as she could care, if it never rang she would be just fine with it.

Tomorrow was Thanksgiving and there were nineteen coming to dinner to eat at the house. They were mostly friends of Ben's and Austin's, but she knew them and liked most of them. She had promised to bake some pies for the annual event and began pulling out the ingredients for the first batch. She loved to make pumpkin pie even though she couldn't eat it.

The sound of sirens startled her at first and it took her several seconds to realize that it was the phone. When she pulled the phone out, there was a picture of the law firm's logo and Devin's name. She thought about letting it go to voice mail and then realized that she would not know how to retrieve it, so she answered it.

"Ronnie Frey," she said in way of greeting. She knew she was clipped, but didn't care if he got mad or not.

"I thought you'd call and say thank you, or to at least say you got the phone at some point." His voice was soft and his tone held humor that she tried hard to ignore.

"Why would I thank you for a device that means you can call me and talk to me? And you knew it was received; one of my roommates signed for it at one-thirty six this afternoon."

He was quiet for so long, she nearly hung up. She really didn't want to speak to him anyway, so if he hung up — great!

"I'm at my mother's house until tomorrow. If you need anything, I want you to call me. How were work and your classes today?"

"I wasn't late to either place and I managed to get through the entire day without having sex with any more than a dozen or so men. I just don't know how I did it. I'm so relieved that your secretary is female, aren't you?"

"Listen, Veronica, I shouldn't have—"

"If there is nothing you'd like to discuss about my working for you, then good-bye, Mr. Grant. I have things to do, men to seduce, and pies to bake—you know, my list is just endless."

"No, nothing. Have a nice Thanksgiving."

Ronnie ended the call without acknowledging him or his salutation.

~~~

Devin closed his phone just as Morgan walked into the study where he had gone to speak to Ronnie.

He nearly snarled at her to go away, but he knew two things about her. One, she would kick his ass if he even tried. Secondly, everyone else in the house would kick it as well. Instead, he said nothing as she sat across from him on the huge couch and looked at him.

"So...you going to tell me what you did to her or do I have to go call her and ask her what you did to her?" That is what he loved about Morgan. She never beat around the bush when going straight through worked better every time.

He stared at her; he was sure with an open-mouthed expression. She grinned and he sat back more into the plush couch. He loved this woman with all his heart and would do anything for her. But right now, he was not above strangling her.

"I'm not even going to ask you why you assume I did anything wrong to her, which I did not, by the way. But I have to ask, what would you ask her if you were to call?"

"Unlike you Grant men, we women who love you know how to resolve matters. You are sitting in here stewing about whatever it is you think you didn't do or should have said or might have done to her, when really all you need to do is to say 'I'm sorry and I love you' then shut up. If I were to call her, I would tell her that she's right, that, while you're cute, you're wrong, then see if she wants to go shopping with me."

He burst out laughing. "Oh, Morgan, why couldn't you have married me instead of my dumbass brother, Nicky?"

"Because, Devin dear, while I love you dearly, you'd make me have to hurt you too often to enjoy it. Seriously, what happened between you and your waitress?"

"Veronica, and don't worry about it, love. It just wasn't meant to be, I suppose," he told her sadly.

They talked about her business, Pink Bag Creations, for a little while. It was an Internet service that set up and then maintained a web based business for people. She had started it before the twins were born and had done very well for herself with it. When one of the twins started to fuss, she left to go and take care of him.

Devin stared at the fire and thought about the next several weeks and working with Veronica. He knew she would avoid him and they would probably fight daily about everything when they did come together. But he just could not believe she hadn't told him about the other men in her life.

Devin knew one thing about Veronica. He knew without a doubt that he was in love with her. Had been, he thought, since the moment she stood up to him in the restaurant all those weeks ago. He just didn't know what the hell he was supposed to do about it. And he didn't know if he really wanted to be in love with her, but he was. It did, however, piss him off.

Caroline had told him Ronnie had been at the office when she had gotten to work at eight-fifteen. Once she had shown Ronnie her new office, she had not come out once. Caroline had checked on Ronnie a few times and had found her on the floor with several of the new law books he had purchased for her spread out all around her. Ronnie had been crawling from one to the next.

Caroline also told him that she liked Ronnie and thought they would suit as partners. When she winked at him, Devin wasn't sure if she meant law partners or personally. He decided not to ask.

Then when he had shown up just as Ronnie was leaving, Caroline had handed him two of the four cases he had coming up and relayed what Ronnie had told her about the information she had found for each case. He wondered, not for the first time, why everyone assumed that he was always the bad guy.

Veronica had gone over each case, made extensive notes in her neat handwriting, and put all the case references on sticky notes about previous rulings and case studies. They were meticulous and orderly. Her notes were concise and, with them, he knew he would have no problems winning both cases.

When she graduated, she was going to be a foe to contend with, he thought, already realizing she would not work for him. He smiled when he thought about being on opposite sides with her and knew that he would have to be on his best game when he did. If he was not, she would rip him to shreds.

Devin got up and threw another log on the fire and thought about the flames that had sparked from her eyes when she had come the other night. His cock hardened at the thought of her screams as she released and the way she had laid on his shoulder sated.

Her body was so responsive and she held nothing back when she came. He had gotten the most pleasure he had ever had with a woman watching her, her face flushed with need, her nipples poking hard against her blouse. When he had nuzzled her breast and found it unfettered from a bra, he had nearly thrown her on the seat and ripped the material from her skin. Biting her had made her fall over the edge and watching her shudder and spasm over and over had nearly been the end of him as well.

But her face was what had captured him; her eyes had darkened to almost black and her cheeks had flushed to a bright red. The sweat trickling down her cheek had even been sexy to him. He wished then that he had tasted her, ran his tongue deep into her heat. He wanted to know if her cream was as delicious as it smelled, heavy and spicy wet.

Christ, he thought, he was hard again and no relief in sight unless he wanted to take care of it himself. But he knew that it would be less than satisfying, a relief short lived, and that was all. He wanted to bury himself inside of her, deep, hard and slow. He wanted her to come over his cock, this time so that he could feel her juices flow over him. Devin groaned when he thought about her body, her small frame, long legs, full breasts and hard nipples. His cock ached and he had to adjust himself again before he sat down and hurt himself.

At one-thirty in the morning, he went up to bed. He thought about taking a cold shower, but simply went to bed instead. It was a long day tomorrow and a shower did not sound very conducive to getting to sleep immediately. So Devin went to bed disappointed, hard, and pissed. He tossed and turned most of the night when he was not dreaming of a beautiful woman with deep purple eyes and pouty, full lips.

~*Chapter 9*~

Thanksgiving preparations were in full swing when Devin finally stumbled downstairs at noon. His mother gave him a reproachful look, but said nothing as he poured himself some coffee and waited at the counter for the caffeine to kick in. But his brothers were not so kind.

From the time Spencer started digging him until just before dinner Devin was the subject of every jibe and poke they could think of. He had been in a horrific mood before he had come down, and by night, he was ready to murder any and all of them.

When Nicky leaned over as he was fixing a plate for his son and asked Devin about his plans for the charity event the next evening, Devin nearly snarled at him, but one look from his mother and he decided that he had better hold his tongue.

"Shit! I forgot about it. I guess I have to go stag. Mom is going to make me pay for this by making me spend more, isn't she?" Devin groused.

"Oh yeah. Remember that first year I went alone? I think I ended up spending nearly ten grand before she would smile at me. I resolved never to let that happen again." Nicky looked over at his wife and winked. Devin avoided looking at Morgan for fear of what she may say about his waitress.

~~~

Ronnie stood in front of the large antique mirror and stared at herself—or at least the woman reflected back at her in the glass. Ben had not let her see her dress until he had presented her with it today, having made it especially for her to wear tonight. The dress was beautiful and it made her feel like she could be as well.

Without any straps, the gown molded and formed to her body like a glove. The bodice was tight and pushed her breasts up, giving them a fuller look, and the single snowflake necklace she wore on a gold chain hung just above her ample cleavage. At her ears hung snowflakes that matched the one at her throat. Turning slightly, she looked at the back.

The back of the gown was low and had laces that started at her spine and worked up to just under her shoulder blades. At her hips, the black material flared into a filmy froth of silk and lace that rested just on top of her toes in the black high heels. The front of the dress had been beaded with black and white seed pearls and shaped into snowflakes that shimmered in the light of the bedroom and would be dazzling in the ballroom. Turning back around, she looked at what Ben had done to her hair and wondered with a grin if he would be willing to do that every morning for the rest of her life.

He had pulled most of her hair into a large pony tail at the back of her head and then taken all the surrounding hair and braided it around her head in a thick, continuous plait. When he had finished with that, he had taken the rest of her hair and had rolled it into intricate curls that hung down her back to the middle. Before he let her see it, tiny snowflakes that had been hand made for her had been stuck into her braid and the curls, giving her a sexy, Christmassy look. Finally, her hose and shoes.

The stockings were thigh-highs that, while black, also shimmered with sparkles and made her legs look twice as long. The heels were a simple black, but at the toe was a bejeweled snowflake that peeked out when she stepped. Smiling and feeling good for the first time in weeks, she grabbed her wrap and tiny purse and walked to the living room to see what her men thought.

"Christ, Ronnie. I could almost become heterosexual if all women looked like you. Honey, you look amazing," Austin told her.

"Isn't it beautiful? Ben, you did such a wonderful job. Everyone is going to wonder where this came from. And I can't wait to tell them. I feel like a million bucks."

She swirled around again and let them see her stockings, which she thought were the cutest thing.

"Ronnie, please tell me that you don't have a gun attached to your leg. Honey, I doubt very much anyone is going to try and...you know, maybe you're right. Dressed like that, you will probably need it to keep the men off you without me there to protect you."

She blushed, knowing that Ben was teasing her. They were both trying to cheer her up and she loved them all the more for it.

The limo pulled up at ten minutes till five o'clock and the both she and Austin went to the door. She wished that Ben could go with them, but with his leg in a cast, he wanted to stay home. Ronnie was sure that he had worn himself out helping her get dressed today, but she also knew that he had enjoyed dressing her as much as she loved him helping. He had even done her makeup for her, tsking the whole time about dark circles that he hoped the light makeup could hide.

The ride to the Polaris Center was about an hour long, but it seemed to fly by for the couple in the car. Austin had told her stories of past events and the reasons why he no longer attended such things. He had been ostracized by the art communities because of his sexual preference and had not returned until this year.

"Why now? I mean, not that I mind going with you, but why this event this year?" she asked him.

"There's someone here I want to meet. I've been following his work for years and I've heard that one of his premier pieces is going to be auctioned off this year. I have some of his other pieces and I want this one. It's said to be one of his best works yet."

"You brought one of your own with you, I noticed. Why?" She knew which piece he had brought. A painting of a young woman lying in a field of heather that he had painted quite a few years ago. It was a gorgeous painting and she liked it.

Austin was a world renowned painter himself and his work went for thousands of dollars on the open market. The resale value of some of his earlier work went for tens of thousands of dollars both in the United States and abroad. But she could understand his passion and his love for art. He had taught her a great deal in the years she had lived with them.

"I hope to be able to donate it tonight to be auctioned off. I have in the long past made donations, but have not done it for a very long time. And this is for a good cause and I can't help but want to contribute. You of all people know how much this particular charity means to me."

She did too. The fight against child abuse was very dear to the three of them—her more than the two of them.

The limo slid to a smooth halt in front of the well lit building and Austin was helped out by the driver. Then Austin reached in for her. She was so nervous that she could feel her palms sweating inside her elbow length gloves. Reaching for his hand, she let him pull her out of the car and into the limelight of the night.

Cameras were everywhere, flashing and pushing in front of them. Reporters were asking questions of them—who they were, why they were there. But neither of them said anything. Ronnie smiled at them and waved as Austin made arrangements with the driver to have someone bring his painting inside and put in the dining area where the auction was being held. Finally, they were moving inside and she was glad for his arm around her waist.

The room had been turned into a fairytale Christmas story. There were several trees around the room all decorated with shiny ornaments and pretty packages with big bows. Each tree had a theme. She could see three of them from where they stood and they each depicted a different Christmas tale. The one directly in front of them was the Nutcracker Suite and the trees were filled with all the characters from the play. The one just beyond was decorated with old fashioned ornaments that looked like something out of the Charles Dickens novel A Christmas Carol. When she saw the tiny crutches and the large geese hanging there, she knew she had guessed correctly.

The tables were round with eight chairs around it. Each table had a small tree in the center that had been decorated as well, including lights and a tiny star atop. Every place setting was marked with a name plate that was attached to a large candy cane and a festive ribbon.

There were waiters and waitresses dressed in black pants and red and white striped shirts seating everyone as they came in. Ronnie could see a large open area and thought it was for dancing later. She forgot to be nervous for a while and just simply enjoyed the atmosphere.

Their table was near the front. She had overheard someone say that the more someone donated, the closer to the front they were. She had no idea how much Austin had given, but she knew that it had been more than she made in the past year.

Most people assumed that she lived with them for free. She probably could, but she did not. She'd paid them rent every month since she had turned eighteen. And aside from the occasional loan to help her with books or fees, she did not take anything from them nor expect it. They would gladly have paid for her education, but this was something she wanted to do on her own.

Ronnie had worked her way through college on her own, odd jobs, and even taking on a couple of tutor jobs to help out. She had gotten a few grants and had won a partial scholarship, but law school was expensive. It was costing her almost fifteen thousand a year to go to school and she was determined that she would not owe anyone anything when she graduated. By this April, she would have her results back from taking her bar exam on January sixth and then she could finally not go to class for a change.

Dinner had just been cleared away with the announcement that the auction would begin in an hour and an area had been cleared the way for the band to start playing. Neither Ronnie nor Austin danced, but they both enjoyed watching the others on the floor. Ronnie was impressed by all the colors of the women's dresses and the men dressed in tuxedos.

"Darling, have I told you how lovely you look this evening? You do, you know. Spectacular, as a matter of fact."

Ronnie turned to look at Austin and grinned. She knew that he wanted something and she would make sure he got it, no matter what it was. There was very little she would not do for either of them.

"Yes, you have. Now tell me what it is you need for me to do for you." They both laughed.

"You're not going to like it, but I would consider it a huge favor to me if you did. You know I don't like to meet people, so I was wondering if you could go find my artist for me? I've seen his name on the list, so I know he's here. Please, Ronnie, it would mean so much to me."

"Of course. You don't need to beg, though you do it very nicely. Who is it and where is he seated?"

He flushed and she suddenly knew that something was up. She just realized that all the times she had asked about the mystery artist, he had never mentioned his name. She knew that she was going to regret it as soon as he would not look her in the eye.

"His name is Grant. Byron Grant. I believe he is related to your Devin Grant somehow. I thought I could go and find him, but I just can't, love."

Ronnie turned away from him and looked at the brightly lit tree. It seemed not quite so bright now, but it could have been the tears in her eyes. She heard Austin say her name, but she waved him off for the moment.

"Tell me where they are seated and I'll go find him for you. I don't know if I'm such a good choice to send to find him, especially if Mr. Grant is still there, but for you, I will try."

He did not say anything for long moments. She thought he was going to tell her not to do it. But even if he did, she would do it for him. Austin and Ben had saved her life and if this was the only thing he asked of her, she would do it.

"They are in the front about six tables to our right. I don't know what he looks like, but I do know that he is young, around thirty, I suppose. Ronnie, don't do this. I'm an ass for even asking you to. Let's go home to Ben."

She stood up and smoothed her dress down her hips and smiled. "I've never been dressed up before around him. Maybe he won't know who I am. I'll be right back."

Taking a deep breath, she turned and headed to the table, hoping that no one would know who she was.

~*Chapter 10*~

Byron watched the woman come toward them again. So far, she had turned back three times before giving herself what looked like a stern talking to and started back again. He was not sure why he thought she was headed for their table, but he knew in his gut she was. He was suddenly very glad his date for the night had left for the ladies room. He did not have to feel guilty ogling this vision before him.

As soon as she was within a couple of feet of the table, he stood. His mother had taught them all manners and this was one time he was very glad of his. From his vantage point, he was getting a very delicious view of the most beautiful breasts he had ever seen. He heard other chairs scrape across the floor and knew that his brothers had seen her too.

"Hello, Ms. Frey. You look very lovely this evening. I don't believe I've seen a more beautiful dress tonight." Byron looked at his mother and nearly swallowed his tongue. This was Devin's waitress!

"Thank you, Mrs. Parker. I'm here to see if I could talk to Mr. Byron Grant about a friend of mine, please." She looked at first him, then Damon, and then back at their mother.

"He doesn't need a date; he has one. But I guess that wouldn't bother you either, would it, Veronica?" Byron watched as she stiffened and paled. Devin might well have hit her for the pain he had apparently caused her by his words.

"Devin Kyle Grant! You'll apologize to her this instant. How dare you speak to someone like that in front of me?"

"I'm sor...it's all right. I...this was a mistake. Forgive me for intruding on your evening, Mrs. Parker." With a quick nod, she turned and left, but headed in the opposite direction she had come from.

Byron sat down with his brothers and waited until his date returned before speaking. He had never been so shocked and angry in his life. It mattered little what she had done to Devin, if anything, but to be spoken to like that in front of strangers was beyond rude. When Alison returned, he told her he needed to speak to someone. He looked at Devin as he stood.

"You are a prick and an asshole, Devin. I never thought I'd say this to one of my brothers before, but I have never been more ashamed of you in my entire life. Mom, I'll be back."

He heard his mom saying something to Devin, but he didn't care. He made his way to the ladies room, where he figured Ronnie had gone.

It was perhaps five minutes before she emerged, and he felt horrible for her all over. Her eyes were puffy and her nose a little red, but she still looked stunning. When she saw him, she looked around, panicky.

"I'm Byron Grant and I'm alone. I left the ass at the table to be dealt with by Mom. I would like to apologize to you on behalf of my family. We are going to have Devin committed when we get home. We don't let him out much, for obvious reasons."

She smiled gently at him and he felt his heart break. This poor woman looked like someone had just run over her favorite toy and then laughed at her tears. But her smile was breathtaking and he decided he would love to see it more.

"You should go back, Mr. Grant. I'm sure my friend will understand. He is well aware of my ongoing issues with your brother. I should have known that he was still pissed. I don't even know what I did to make him hate me so much. "

"I'm not going back until I help you out. It's the least I can do for what...you know, for right now, I don't have a brother. Tell me what you need. Please, Ms. Frey, it would be my pleasure."

He could see her struggle with her indecision. He liked her all the more for not wanting to come between families. But, finally, she just blurted out what had sent her to their table, or at least who.

"I have a friend who would like to meet you. He has been your greatest fan for years and has quite a few pieces of your work. He had heard you were going to be here tonight and has come out of seclusion to be here. He just wants to shake your hand and talk to you. It shouldn't take long, if you're sure."

"Of course, I would love to meet him. I'm always excited to meet a fan. I stay so far removed sometimes trying to hit deadlines that I seldom get to see people anymore." She started back the way she had come and he made sure he was on her left so that she would not have to look at the table where his family was currently berating Devin.

"Yes, he has the same problems. But he is working less these days and is enjoying himself. But I think he is starting to miss it a little and I expect to see him at it again soon."

87

Byron looked up at the table she had indicated with a wave of her arm. He stood stock still and looked at the man at the table who was starting to rise from his seat. Christ, his idol!

"You're Austin Pride! Holy shit! Austin Pride. When she said someone wanted to...holy shit, it's you! Austin Pride wants to meet me."

"Well, I guess you two know each other," Ronnie said with laughter in her voice. She was smiling again and Byron smiled back.

Byron could not help himself; he grabbed Ronnie by her shoulders and pulled her to him for a kiss. He was so happy that he did not notice her look of shock and her obvious embarrassment. Austin Pride wanted to meet him.

"I've been following your work since your first show. You were an incredible artist then, but you have improved greatly in the ensuing years. I've wanted to meet you for years," Austin told him.

Ronnie sat down to Austin's left and when he looked at her, she shook her head. Byron knew then that she had only come to their table because this man had asked her to. Then he remembered some of the things Devin had been saying today and realized that he did not know what the hell he was talking about. He knew enough about the sensitive nature of this man's relationship with the art world and why he had dropped out of sight for so long.

"My brother is an ass, Mr. Pride, and I fear he hurt Ms. Frey very badly when she came to get me. I would like to say that I'm sorry. And he will be too when we get home tonight."

"Don't, Mr. Grant. Please don't. He'll think what he wants no matter what you say to him. It doesn't matter anyway. I'll know Monday if I passed the exam to test out of the class I'm taking, then I'll be finished with school. I no longer have any need of an internship and will be out of his hair soon enough. Then I'll take my bar exam later next month so I'll just have to wait and see. So, you see, I'm not worth you being mad at him over. But I do thank you for your concern." Ronnie hurried with her statement, but Byron could hear the hurt in her voice.

Byron wondered if Devin knew this and decided he would not tell him. He deserved to lose out on her. Hell, maybe he would ask her out. But he knew that she would turn him down. Even he could see that she loved Devin, the ass.

"I have something I'd like to donate before it gets too much later—a painting that I did several years ago. I know that I should have contacted someone sooner, but I didn't know of the reception I would receive if I did. Would you like to see it first?" Austin told Byron as he waved one of the servers over to help.

"Yes, of course." Byron knew that even if his mother did not want to put it up because the list had already been made, he would buy it and donate the money. He had quite a few Pride paintings and was always ready to add more to his collection.

Ronnie helped the server pick up the wrapped package and peeled the tape off the back and gently pulled it off the front to reveal the painting beneath.

Byron leaned forward and then looked at Austin. He nearly said something and stopped by the quick shake of the older man's head. He looked back at the painting and knew that he was going to purchase it. And it mattered little to him what it would cost. It was simply beautiful—as beautiful as the subject matter was.

"Ronnie, love, do you think you could get me a glass of wine? And please get Mr. Grant here one as well. You know how men are when they need to grunt over a piece of art or a feetball game?"

"Yes, and its football, not feet. I'll be back. Will thirty minutes be long enough for you to talk about the painting?" She stood and kissed Austin on his cheek. When she darted a quick glance at the direction of his table, Byron wanted to go and pound Devin again.

As soon as she was out of earshot, Byron asked, "It's her, isn't it? And she doesn't know it."

"Yes, it's Ronnie when she turned twelve. She sees the same thing you do, a very beautiful child in a field of heather. The only difference is, you see the little girl I painted and she doesn't."

"Have you told her? No, I can see that you haven't. And even if you did, she wouldn't believe you. Are there anymore of her?"

"You are a very clever man. Yes, there are two more. One I will never part with and the other is still wet, and I haven't decided the fate of that one yet. The first one I painted of her, she was about nine or so. It's my favorite piece I've ever done. She is sitting in a large chair that we have since gotten rid of reading Sun Tzu on The Art of War and understanding it. Ben, my partner, decided she was much too smart for the crap they had been reading in class and took her to the library. She came home with that and several others, including Lady Chatterley's Lover that he had bought in a used bookstore on the way home. I believe she may still have that copy somewhere."

Byron laughed with him and looked back at the painting. He wanted it now more than before. The story with this one had to be just as entertaining and he could not wait to hear it.

90

"And this one? Why a field of heather?" Byron was already thinking where to put it when he got it home.

Austin looked lovingly at the painting and told him why. "Ronnie came from an abusive childhood. If you don't know that already, then I'm sure you'll hear about it. I'm not sure of all the details, but for the most part, she ran away when she was just a child. I found her one night sleeping behind a dumpster having a nightmare. She had been eight at the time and nearly starved and frozen cold. I brought her home with me and Ben and I cleaned her up. The scars that child had would make you cry, and not just from the physical abuse either. It took us nearly six months to get her to trust us even slightly. And longer still to get her to tell us her name. We never formally adopted her, not that we could back then. We just told people she was our sister's child and we were caring for her. Then when she was twelve, a man showed up out of nowhere and demanded his daughter back. Of course, we knew it was her father; she had told us enough about him that we knew it had to be him. We denied knowing Ronnie. I can't remember now what he called her, but it wasn't what she had told us. After he left, we went in search of her. She was in the park, lying just how you see her in a bed of heather. When Ben asked her why she had hidden there, she said that if she was going to die this time by his hand, she wanted to be able to smell the pretty flowers while she died. It broke our hearts. Our relationship changed after that. She became our child then. I think it was because she believed then that we would not give her up. I love that child as though she was of my blood, and so does my Ben."

In the end, Austin gave the painting to Byron. They had shared more than a budding friendship over a charity dinner, and both men were better for it. They both loved the child that had grown into a lovely woman as well. Byron also knew that he would not help Devin win the girl's love, but would be there if he needed him.

Ronnie showed up a few minutes later with two glasses of wine. Byron stayed for a few minutes more, and then went back to his table with the painting. The men had exchanged numbers and addresses and Byron was happy that he had followed Ronnie to the ladies room.

After making arrangements to have the painting put into his car, he went back to his table a much happier man. Of course, he was also poorer. He wrote his mother a check for the painting and told her he would explain later. Yes, he was much happier, he decided.

~~~

Devin went home right after the dinner. He had made an ass of himself and as much as he wanted to blame Ronnie, he knew that he could not. He had been cruel to her and he had done so publicly. His mother was really mad at him and he was sure one or all of his brothers wanted to knock the shit out of him. Except for Byron, who had been unnaturally quiet when he came back to the table and had not stopped smiling. He wanted to call Ronnie and tell her he was sorry, but he still could not help but think about the other men in her life, and he was also afraid his brother was becoming one of her lovers.

By Sunday afternoon after spending two miserable days by himself, Devin had come to the decision that he would not go near Ronnie again. If she wanted to call him Mr. Grant, then so be it. He would give her the case files he needed, make sure she knew when she was to appear in court with him, and not worry if she did not show up. He was going to move on. He was not going to look at her, not going to want her, and he certainly was not going to touch her.

On Monday morning, that all went to shit as soon as he saw her walking into her office.

Devin hid out in his office until nearly noon when he was sure she was gone. Then felt stupid because he had. His name was on the door, for crying out loud, and he should be able to go where he wanted when he wanted. Caroline met him at her desk as he was going to lunch.

"Mr. Grant, here are the cases you left for Ronnie. They are all complete, including the ones you messaged me about over the weekend. I also have a message here from the State Law Board that asks if her test results come here, or were we aware if she had another firm that she was going to work for. I told him you would call him back as I didn't know what he meant."

He took the message and frowned at the name. He knew Richard Douglas. They had gone to law school together. He went back into his office to call.

"Hey, big guy. So, how is life treating the rich and famous Grant brothers? I heard your brother Nick got married recently."

"Yeah, a couple of years ago. You'd like Morgan, she's great. What is this about Veronica Frey's test results? I thought I had a month before I had to set that up for her."

As her boss, he had thought he would sign her up for the two day exam and make sure the results were sent to whoever she wanted. Normally, it took several months to get the results back and Devin was not sure what was going on.

"Hey, now there's a looker for you. Damn if she isn't the finest thing I've ever seen on a pair of long legs. But as a married man, I can only look and dream. Let me find her file."

Devin was just glad they were not face to face because he was reasonably sure that he would have hit the other man for his comments about his woman. He did not even try and correct himself in his thinking that she was not his woman this time and just pretended he didn't hear himself. He was in deep and he was only just realizing how deep.

"Okay, says here she took an opt-out test for her last class on Wednesday and the results were given to her...this morning. She became eligible to take the state test immediately and her former boss, hummm, Judge Stone had it set up that she could take it even if it wasn't being offered. I thought she was taking the exam tomorrow morning, but let me check."

Devin was shocked. And angry. How could she do this to him? Then he remembered he had given her every reason to do this to him. He had done nothing but make her life a living hell since he had first seen her. And for every part of him that wanted to pull her close, just as much of him wanted to push her away. His head began to hurt and he rubbed his forehead as he waited for Richard to return.

"Here is it. No, I'm sorry, she's taking the exam next week. On Monday and Tuesday. The reason we've called is because she listed herself as your intern, but she didn't mark to send the results to you, only to her home address. We tried contacting her, but there is no answer and she didn't give us a cell phone number. Do you know how to get in touch with her and find out?"

Yes, Devin thought, he would get in touch with her and wring her pretty neck, right after he nibbled on it for a while. After telling Richard he would get back to him, he tried her cell. She was not answering and he didn't leave a message.

At two o'clock, he went to lunch, but made sure Caroline knew to contact him if Ronnie called in or came in. He kept trying as well. By the time he had left the office, he had left her forty-one messages and had called her house about that many times. He was going by there on his way home and hell would be paid when he found her.

~*Chapter 11*~

Devin pulled up in front of her home just as two men were getting out of a nice late model Mercedes. He did not figure them for her roommates because these men looked to be in their late fifties.

"May I help you?" The man walking on crutches turned to ask him. The other man just smiled and went to the door of the house with bags of what appeared to be groceries.

"I'm looking for Veronica Frey. She's not answering her phone and I—"

"And you're pissed because she isn't doing what you want. Hello, Devin. I'm Ben and this is Austin. You'd better come inside. You're not going to be any happier once we tell you what happened to her."

Devin's heart skipped several beats. Ben had said "what happened to her," implying something had. Austin came back out before Devin could move and shoved a bag into his arms to get him going.

"Here, make yourself useful. And you will behave in my house, young man, or I'll rip your head off and pike it outside with the Christmas lights for everyone to see. Understand me? Ben and I are stressed about this enough without you adding to the mix."

"Is she all right? Where is she?" Austin's snarled voice did nothing to calm his nerves.

"Hospital. Come inside, I'm not discussing this outside in the flipping cold where everyone who wants to can hear."

Hospital. Devin didn't know if he collapsed or what, but he was suddenly on the ground. Austin was fanning him with a box of graham crackers, the kind with cinnamon, his mind registered. Ben was shouting something about calling nine-one-one.

"I'm fine. I'm sorry, is she all right?" Devin found that he didn't just want to know if she was all right, but he needed to know.

"Yes. She was mugged. Damned girl actually...let's get you inside, Devin. I think we both could use a drink," Austin said as he helped Devin to his feet.

Next thing Devin knew, he was sitting in a huge living room in a deep leather chair and Austin was handing him a short glass of amber liquid with a single cube of ice. Devin's first sip confirmed that not only was it bourbon, but a very good brand as well.

"I'd like to call my brother Damon to have him go and look in on her. He's a top rated physician."

"The doctor we have watching her is top rate as well. Did you expect us to do anything less for her? She's our child and we would move heaven and earth for her."

Devin looked at Ben as he spoke. Child? Then he looked at the other man who was looking at Ben with love and affection in his eyes. Suddenly, it dawned on him. Veronica had never called them anything but roommates, but they were so much more — to each other and to her.

"You're partners, not her lovers," he said. Realization hit him hard at right around his heart. Would she ever be able to forgive him? he wondered.

"Very good. Now I bet you can figure out the rest too if you just shut up and think before you speak," Austin said.

Devin noticed the snarl in the older man's tone again and knew he deserved it. But he was worried about her as well and was willing to take anything these men gave him just to know she was all right.

"She really is all right. They're keeping her over night because of the bump on her head. Stupid girl is going to bite off more than she can chew one of these days. To think of her and that brute of a man...oh, Austin, our poor little girl."

"She's all right, Ben. That's all that matters, and she'll be back in the morning, provided she behaves herself while in the hospital," Austin said gently to his partner.

Devin took a large gulp of his bourbon. "What happened? So far all I know is she's got a bump and she's in the hospital. Please, I need to know."

"She was Christmas shopping and when she had finished, she was waiting for the damned bus, which was late again. I don't know why she won't let us just buy her a new car instead of pouring money into that piece of crap she drives." Ben looked a little pissed at that, and Austin nearly grinned.

"Because she owns it, and owing us, even though she loves us, goes against her pride for some reason. Go on, love. Tell him the story without embellishments, please." Austin said to his lover.

"Anyway, some man tried to grab the woman next to Ronnie's purchases and when she stepped in, he decided to take hers as well—major mistake on his part. Ronnie flew at him like a woman with PMS. I don't think the man knew what hit him. But the time the police showed up, he was begging for them to take him away."

Devin could see her do it too, the crazy woman. When he got a hold of her, he was going to set down a few rules. And then thought he might want to suggest a few rules with a wary grin. But paddling her butt was becoming more and more appealing every time he thought about her.

"But you said she was mugged. What happened then if she took care of the would-be robber?"

"The woman next to Ronnie. It was a ruse, you see. The man would try and take his partner's things and when no one was looking, she'd make off with the goods of the people around her. Problem is they didn't expect their target to have a black belt, nor that she would give chase. Ronnie got hit in the head by her cell phone when the woman turned and threw it at Ronnie. Caught her just to the corner of her left eye and knocked her out. Ronnie was damned lucky the car coming around the same corner only ran over her phone and not her."

Well, he thought, that explained why he couldn't get in touch with her all day. His list of reasons to strangle the woman was growing exponentially. But so were his reasons for kissing her until she could not speak. Not speaking was something he was going to practice, himself, for a change.

Devin stared into the fireplace. He knew he had been doing that a lot lately. He had a lot on his mind and knew he needed to share with someone or go insane.

"She hates me. Not that I blame her, but she does. Something I'm going to tell you is something I've only just discovered recently and I've never even said out loud. I love her. I think I have from the moment I first met her."

"She's very easy to love, but not easy to get to know. Trust me when I tell you, we've been trying for years to have her open up to us. You two have some things to work out, I believe." Austin glanced at Ben, and then continued. "She's in room four-twelve. It's a private room. She not going to be happy because we told you, but she'll forgive us, especially if you do this right. Don't push her, Devin. She's terrified of becoming her father and hitting you first the other night and now this man has her depressed about it. You've read her file, she said, so you know what I'm talking about."

"I deserved it as much as the other man did. Hell, probably more so. I wasn't a very nice man to her and I plan to make up for it."

"She won't see it that way. She'll see that she hurt you by violence and nothing else. For all her bravo, she is a very insecure little girl inside."

Thirty minutes later, Devin was parking in the big lot at OSU hospital. It was after visiting hours, but a quick call to Damon and he had permission to stay until he left, or Ronnie kicked him out—which Damon thought would happen. Damon was also going to check on Ronnie in the morning before she left. It was nine-thirty when he knocked on her door.

"Go away before I call security." Not a good beginning, he thought, but he was determined. He laid the dozen red roses on the small table and noticed that there were several vases of flowers all around the room, including one from Byron. Figures Byron would know she had been hurt before him.

"I heard about what happened. I stopped by and spoke to Austin and Ben when I couldn't get in touch with you. Nice couple, by the way."

Her grunt made him smile, but he quickly covered it with a stern look. This was no time to be smiling at her.

"What the hell were you thinking taking on someone twice your size? Do you have a death wish?" Her eye was swollen almost shut and it looked to have four stitches.

"Go away!" She yelled at him and then took a pillow from behind her and tossed it at him. He caught it and started walking toward her.

He stood staring down at her for several seconds when he realized how tired he was. Not just tired, but exhausted. He took off his coat and tossed it into the nearby chair. Next, he took off his tie and tossed it as well. They both watched as it slid to the floor in a pile of blue silk. His jacket was next and joined the growing number of garments he tossed carelessly toward the chair. When he reached for his belt buckle, Ronnie spoke up.

"What do you think you're doing? Put those things back on and get out of here." He noticed her voice had become husky and low. The sound shot straight to his cock and he felt a surge of need pour into him. This woman made him feel things he didn't even know he wanted to feel.

The belt came off with a bit of flair and he didn't watch where it landed, but looked at the woman he loved. Before he said anything, he started unbuttoning his shirt.

"I've not slept well over the past few days and I—"

"That's my fault, I suppose," Ronnie snarled at him.

"Yes and no. Most of it is my fault, though some of the blame lies on your doorstep. You could have told me that Austin and Ben were not your lovers, Veronica." He toed off his left shoe as he spoke.

"I don't have to explain myself to you, Mr. Grant. Why are you undressing?" She started to pull the blankets tighter around her. He thought it would do her no good.

"No, you didn't. Not before, at any rate. Especially in light of the way I've treated you." The shirt came off and he folded it and laid it on the chair as he toed off his other shoe. "As for undressing, I can't sleep in my clothes. I usually sleep in the raw, but because of where we are, I'll leave my pants on. Now, scoot over and give me some room."

He didn't wait for her to comply, which he knew she would not anyway, but simply moved in behind her on the narrow bed and pushed her over and on to her side. The hospital gown had ridden up somewhat and before he pulled the blanket over them both, he got the nicest view of her bare bottom covered only by a thin string that separated the muscled orbs. His cock jumped in response.

She was quiet for so long that he thought she might be all right with him there, but should have known better. When she flipped over and glared down at him from her sitting position, he knew the true meaning of need. Her breasts heaved in her anger and her warm hip pressed against his thigh, her heat seeping into him even through his heavy pants.

When she jerked her side of the blankets off her and made to slid off the bed, he moved quickly and pinned her back to the bed, her arms held above her head with his hand and her legs anchored beneath his. Just to show her what she was doing to him and his libido, he pressed hard into her.

"I'm tired. Very tired, but if you continue to tempt me, I'm going to make love to you right here. Now lay still and to go sleep. My brother will be here in the morning and I'd like to be rested when he comes in. He and the rest of my family is very upset with me and I'm pretty sure if I make love to you right now, we will still be doing it when he arrives in the morning. Now, roll over so I can hold you properly."

Moving her to her side so that he could spoon himself at her back proved to be easier than he thought it would be. When he wrapped his arm around her waist, he pulled her closer as his other arm slid under her head. He knew she could feel his cock and when she stiffened and started to pull away, he stopped her with his hand pressed to her belly.

"Don't, baby. I'm not an animal that would take advantage of you while you hurt, no matter what I said earlier. It's just my body's reaction to a very beautiful woman in my arms. Rest, we'll talk tomorrow." Her snort made him laugh a little and he snuggled down into her warmth.

"I hate you right now," she said in a voice so full of hurt he wanted to comfort her in ways he had seen Spencer do for his daughter Meggie.

"I know you do, but we'll talk about that tomorrow as well. Now, go to sleep. I need my strength."

It was a long time coming, but he felt her body begin to relax against his. Soon after, he heard the even tone of her breathing and knew that she had fallen asleep. He felt like the king of the world at that moment.

Closing his eyes, he wondered how long it would be before he would be able to sleep too, and then nothing else as sleep claimed him as well.

~~~

Ronnie woke warm and snuggled deeper into it. When something tightened about her waist, she remembered where she was and, more importantly, who was with her.

The room was still semi-dark and she knew she needed to get out while the man with her was still sleeping. Sometime through the night, she had ended up sprawled over him, her head tucked under his chin, his arms around her waist. She tried to pull away, but he brought her back to him every time. Sliding her leg up between his to try and get some leverage, he grabbed her by the knee and pulled it up over his hip and held her there. His groin rocked into hers and she looked up and into blue eyes.

"Good morning, love. You're very warm." His voice like warm maple syrup poured over her and into every pore of her body. She felt herself melting into him.

"I'm trying to move off you. Please let me go," she said. But instead of letting her go, he rolled her to her back and leaned up and over her. He smiled down at her from above her. Her leg was still wrapped tightly over his hip.

"If you let me kiss you, I'll let your leg go. That is, if you want me to. If you let me hold you while I kiss you, I'll get up — again, if you want me to." His voice was husky and it did all sorts of things to her body.

She stared up at him and considered. She actually liked his body over hers, but that did not mean she was going to tell him that. She just knew that it would be a mistake somehow. And the thought of him kissing her again had her also remembering what had happened the last time he had kissed her and she felt a blush heating her cheeks. His groan made her body respond in ways that made her stiffen with the unfamiliar longings.

But he didn't seem to need an answer as his head slowly lowered to hers. She licked her lips in anticipation of his lips being pressed against hers.

"Veronica, you tempt me. You know that, don't you? Tempt me to want more than a simple kiss."

"There is nothing ever simple about you, Devin. Kiss me, please."

His mouth covered hers and she knew he was going to go beyond a mere kiss. When his tongue slid inside of her mouth to duel with her tongue, she felt her body being pressed harder into the bed from the weigh shifting into her. When she felt his hand release her leg, she didn't move it, but lifted it higher on his hip to press herself tighter to him. His hand brushed her breast and she moaned deep within her chest.

105

Her nipple responded to his bare touch and when he rubbed his thumb over the erect peak, she surged against his hand. His mouth, hot and wet against her mouth, moved down her neck to the place where her shoulder met.

Dizzy now, her body needing his, she touched him, ran her hand along his chest to his belly and then to the top of his pants at the snap.

"Touch me, Veronica. Please, touch me." Hesitantly, she moved her hand lower and brushed her fingers over his rigid, thick cock. When he moved tighter against her, his body trapping her hand between them, she opened her palm over him and pressed back. His growl raced over her skin like a caress and her pussy clenched tightly and wept.

"Please, Devin, help me." She begged him and didn't care that she did. Her body was on fire, on fire for his and what he could do for her.

Shifting again, he moved between her legs and moved fully over her. Ronnie wrapped her bare legs around him and, using his body for leverage, surged hard up against him and his cock, riding him over and over.

A cool breeze, a tiny change in the temperature, distracted her for a moment and then his mouth was over her bare breast, nipping and laving her nipple. Heat like nothing she had every felt filled her. She knew she was close, close to the delicious point he had taken her before, and she wanted it, wanted him.

A knock, loud in the quiet room, startled them. The voice beckoned from beyond hard against the wood.

"Devin? Devin, open up, the door is locked."

Heart pounding, she looked up at the man who was pulling away, her body missing his heat immediately.

"Devin!"

"I'm coming. Just...give me a minute to wake up." He looked down at her again and leaned close to kiss her. "I'm so sorry, love. Christ, you look so tempting laying there with my bite marks on your skin. If I could, I'd send him away, but I know he won't go."

When she started to pull away and right her gown, she wondered how he had managed to get both sleeves undone and have her bare from the waist up so quickly, he stilled her hands with one of his.

"Don't. Please don't push me away. Not now. What we did and we were about to do was something we both wanted. Still want, actually. Let Damon release you and I'll take you home and we'll talk, okay?"

Afraid of what she might say or beg him to do, she nodded. And watched as he moved toward the door, pulling his shirt on but leaving it untucked. He started to take another step then returned and kissed her again.

"Hurry, love, or he'll break the door down and as much as I love your breasts just like they are all rosy from my mouth, I'd rather Damon not see them."

That got her moving and she was completely covered and the blankets over her before Devin open the door to his brother.

~*Chapter 12*~

Devin could tell by the look on his brother's face he knew what he and Veronica had been doing—or at least what they had almost done. Reaching beneath the tails of his shirt, he adjusted his cock again. Christ, he thought, if he got any harder, he would be able to ram nails into a two-by-four with it.

He watched as Damon checked Veronica's eye and was glad when he didn't insist on a blood pressure check before releasing her and telling her to get dressed. He was sure that if she was only half as pumped up as he was, she would be off the charts.

For as much as Devin wanted to stay and help her with her dress, he followed Damon out into the hall when he had motioned for him to go with him.

"If you asked her to stay with her last night just to seduce her into sex, I'll haul your ass out of here so fast—"

"We didn't...I didn't...damn it, Damon. I swear to you it was never my intention. I only wanted to hold her, and then this morning...that was mutual, I swear it. She...I love her, Damon. I would never force her into something...I know I've not given any of you reason to believe me when it comes to her, but I swear, I would never hurt her — not now, not ever."

Damon nodded after a long pause then hugged his brother to him. Devin hadn't realized how much he needed that, not until he was being held. He needed his family as much as he needed Veronica. Now, all he had to do was prove it to her.

"Take her home. She needs to rest. And, Devin, I mean rest. Not with you in the bed with her. That girl looks like she's been kissed all night long and wants more of it. She won't get any proper rest with you doing that to her."

To say that Devin was shocked by his brother's words would have been an understatement, but when Damon smiled and explained, Devin found himself slightly relieved.

"I've been watching those reality shows on television. Some of them are pretty bad, but there are times it's like watching a train wreck, you just can't make yourself look away."

"Yeah, well, maybe you shouldn't say that in front of Mom, or Veronica. I'm pretty sure that one or both of them would hurt you. Mom would more than likely castrate you in a heartbeat for it."

Devin walked back into Ronnie's room just as she was coming out of the bathroom. She looked at everything but him. He wanted to smile at that, but knew that she would hurt him if he did.

"Damon said you could go home. I'll take you. I...I'm not working today." He felt some shyness settle over him. He couldn't remember the last time he had felt this way, if ever.

"I should call Austin. I don't know what he's planning today." She walked over to the phone and before she could pick it up, it rang. She jumped back from it. Both of the laughed. Yeah, they were both acting out of sorts.

It was Austin. She talked to him for a few minutes and Devin could tell that something was wrong, but waited until she hung up before asking. Ronnie looked over at him several times and he walked up behind her. He was not listening in on her conversation; he just needed to touch her. Moving her hair to the side, he began to kiss her neck. When she leaned back against him, he wrapped his arm around her waist and held her there. He didn't realize how much he needed her touch until she hung up the phone and stayed there.

"You have the most unique taste. And your skin is so warm and soft." He bit her gently and then licked the area with his tongue. Her sigh nearly had him bite her again.

"I'm ready to go. I...that feels very good. Will you kiss me again, Devin? Please?" She turned in his arms and looked up at him.

He was surprised by what he saw there. Her eyes were tearing up and she looked so sad. When one of her tears rolled down her cheek, he lifted his hand and wiped it away with his thumb.

"What is it, baby? Why are you crying? Did I do something to upset you?" Devin kissed her gently on her mouth and held her closer to his body.

"No. Nothing like that. I just...I want to go home, please. I'm just really tired, all right?"

He didn't believe her, but pushing her right now didn't seem right. The nurse came in at that moment with Ronnie's discharge papers and he went to get the car. He was about halfway across the lot when his phone rang.

"It's Austin Pride, Devin. I wanted to ask a favor of you. I know we haven't gotten along all that well, but Ronnie is very important to us and I don't want her hurt."

"I would never hurt her, Austin. I would have hoped by now that you'd know that. She means a great deal to me." He parked in another parking space; he didn't want to try and explain himself while trying to drive.

"Yes. I know that. It's just that...we love her very much. And, well, she shouldn't be alone. Not now at any rate. Did you know that she hates Christmas? I don't mean just hates, but if she could be anywhere alone this time of year, she would go. Her father, she said he hurt her on Christmas."

Devin knew that; somewhere in the back of his mind he had registered that she had been hurt on Christmas morning and he had never thought about her reaction to the date before. Then he realized what Austin had said.

"Alone? I don't understand. She just asked me to bring her home. I thought I was taking her to you." He hadn't been listening to her call and now wished that he had.

"No, Ben and I are on our way to the airport. We've had this holiday plan for several weeks now. He and I go to New York every year to shop and catch a few plays. Ronnie usually goes to a very nice hotel as a gift from us to get pampered and relax. While we're all gone, the decorators come in and do up the whole house for the holidays. She didn't tell you?"

"No, she didn't. When does this start? I'm assuming sometime soon." He was beginning to see why she was sad. Alone and hurt was not a good start to a pamper session.

"We're actually debating on whether we should continue on to the airport. I want you to know that we aren't asking you to babysit for us. We would like to know if you'd just, I don't know, just check up on her for us a couple of times? We'll be back on Sunday night. So it wouldn't be all that long, really."

"You have a good time, Austin. I'll take care of her. I'm going to tell...let me rephrase that, I'm going to see if she'll come to my house with me." He knew better than to assume anything or to order her around. She may be hurt right now, but he was sure she could peel a strip off of him wider and quicker than his mother.

"All right. I appreciate this. I guess Ben was right. You aren't so bad after all."

~~~

Ronnie was lying back in the chair when Devin returned with the nurse and the wheelchair. She groaned, but knew that it was hospital policy to have the patient leave this way. Devin looked distracted, but he smiled at her. She started to lean down and tie her other shoe when he was suddenly in front of her patting his thigh. She lifted her foot so that he could tie it for her.

"Are you hungry? I am, starved actually. How about I take you to breakfast before I take you home? We could get something really fattening." He wiggled his brows at her and she burst out laughing.

"All right, but I'm not really very hungry. I...my head hurts a bit and I have a prescription to fill too." Her head actually pounded, but she thought if she said that, they would make her stay.

"Sure. Let's get you in the car; I only have about three more minutes before the security guard said he'd tow me."

By the time they got to the car, Ronnie was slightly nauseous. She closed her eyes against the moving walls and pressed her hand hard against her belly. She thought about begging the nurse to hit her over the head so that she would not have to see.

She stood up next to his open car door and he pulled her into his arms. Nothing had ever felt that good before. She laid her head on his shoulder and started to cry softly.

"Sweetheart, let me get you home. I think once you get some rest, your head will stop spinning. Come on, baby, in you go." She sat down and he picked her legs up and set them in the car.

As the door started to shut, he stopped it suddenly and leaned in to kiss her. The kiss was quick and soft, but she felt it all the way to her toes. For those few seconds, she completely forgot about her head.

He got in on his side and before he put it into gear, he reached across her and pulled the safety belt over her lap. He brushed her breast and she moaned and looked up at him.

Devin's eyes had darkened to almost black and he looked pained. Before she could ask him if he was all right, he buckled her in and put the car into gear and pulled away.

"Veronica, baby, I'm taking you to my house just outside of Columbus. And if you don't want to end up in my bed, naked with me inside of you very soon afterwards, I would suggest that you tell me now. I have never wanted a woman like I do you and every time I touch you, the need gets stronger. So, what's it going to be?" He never took his eyes off the road, but his grip on the steering wheel looked painful.

"I want to go home with you. Austin and Ben are gone, and the house is... I've never had sex before. I'm probably not any good at it anyway. But I thought you should know, you know, just in case that makes a difference to you." She had to clear her throat three times before she finally got it out.

Nothing was said for a few miles. She shifted on her seat and wondered if there was a way for her to open the door and just tumble out into the oncoming traffic. She thought it would be better than sitting here in the dead silence of the car. She had never told anyone she was a virgin. Austin knew, of course, and more than likely Ben, but no one else. She wondered if he thought she was some sort of freak.

"Are you on any sort of birth control?" His voice sounded all husky again and she shifted again in the seat. The things he did to her with his voice, she could only wonder what he would do with is body.

"Yes. I never...that is to say, the thought of sex was...I never...sex was never really a big deal before. I've had...hummm, offers before, but the thought of a man touching me sort of made me...I would throw up mostly."

"You want to throw up when I touch you, Veronica? When I have your nipple in my mouth or my body pressed to yours, do you feel sick then?" She glanced at him. She wondered if he was making fun of her, but didn't think he was.

"No, you don't make me sick. I do feel things when you touch me—things that I know as desire and maybe a need, but I don't really understand them. I'm not stupid. I know what sex is and how all the parts fit together, but reading about it and doing it I don't think are the same." She felt her face heat up and reached to roll down the window for a minute.

"No, they aren't the same. And I know you aren't stupid—you are far from it. This sickness, does it have anything to do with your father? I don't know what happened that day, but I've seen enough cases and talked to Damon enough to know that your dad wasn't as saintly as he professed."

Ronnie looked out the window. No, her father was not saintly—more evil than anything. She wasn't sure what to tell him, but if he wanted to have sex with her, she needed to let him know. It may not have anything to do with him, but she wasn't sure what it would do to her once she and Devin started it.

"If we could please wait to get to your house, I'll tell you everything. If you want to be with me in that way, then you should know what kind of person I come from."

"All right. But, Veronica, it'll matter little to me. I've already fallen in love with you." She didn't say anything. He would probably change his mind soon anyway.

~*Chapter 13*~

"I remember my sisters' third birthday like it was yesterday. They were both dressed in bright pink dresses and their hair was tied back in pink bows, as well. Margo had on white stockings and Holly's were white with tiny hearts on them. She had gotten the heart ones because she had made our father come fastest for two nights in a row."

"Christ," Devin hissed. They were sitting on the couch in his living room. There was a fire in the hearth and the room had been tastefully decorated for Christmas. She looked at his tree and continued.

"I had just finished clearing the table while they had all gone into the living room. My mother was already out; it was late enough in the day that she had had plenty enough to drink. So it was just the three of them." Devin pulled her into his arms and she leaned her back against his chest.

"When was this and how old were you? I know that your sisters were born in November, but your file didn't have anything much about your birth."

"I was four. My birth date is May twenty-sixth. The reason there are no records is because I was born at home. I was told that my mother went into labor with me while my father was at work and by the time he got home, there I was. He told me that since neither of us was dead, there didn't seem to be a reason for him to call in a doctor. I'm not sure if that's the real reason, but it's the only one I know.

"The table was cleared and I was putting the things in the trash when I heard them. This was different than the other times they had sex. I went to the door just as he, my father...they were all naked and my sisters were on either side of him. He was inside of them with his hands, stretching them, he called it. I suppose that was what he was doing. Suddenly, he picked up Margo and put her on his lap. She had done this before and when she saw me looking at her from the door, she stuck out her tongue. The next instance, she was screaming. He had...he impaled her on him. I don't think they had ever gone that far before."

She was crying now. Not for her sister, because for as long as Ronnie had lived there after that day, her sisters had never complained about what he had done. She was crying for the lost innocence that day — both theirs and hers.

"Go on, baby, tell me the rest. What happened next?" She felt his arms tighten around her and she held his arms to her.

"When Margo stopped screaming and was only crying, he rolled her to her back and pumped into her. I couldn't see them at that point, but I could hear him. He kept telling her over and over how tight she was and that she was his special angel. When he threw back his head and shouted out, he saw me. I didn't move, I couldn't move. He stood up when he was finished and turned toward me. I didn't want to look, but I glanced down at his thing—his penis. It was covered in blood. I...I had to grab onto the wall before I passed out while he ran his hand along it, spreading the blood over the end and it got hard again. He lifted Holly by her hair and guided her head to him and she licked him clean. I didn't make it to the bathroom before I started throwing up."

She was sobbing now. In all the years since she had left home, she had never thought of that day and now it came rushing into her like a missile. Devin turned her in his arms and held her close to him, rubbing his hand up and down her back while he kissed her head. She wasn't sure what he was saying, but it was soft and kind and she felt it in her heart.

She must have fallen asleep because when she opened her eyes, she was in a bed with the covers tucked tight around her like a cocoon. She had to struggle for several minutes to get up. Her pants and shoes were off, but her shirt, bra and panties were still on. There was still blood on her shirt and bra from yesterday so she opened the massive closet on the far wall and pulled one of his shirts off the hanger and pulled it on over her panties. The others pieces of clothing she carried with her.

She found him in one of the rooms downstairs. He was on the phone when she walked by and he waved her inside. She didn't know where to go so she sat on the chair across from him. He hung up a minute later.

"How do you feel? I bet you're starving. I was going to order us something, but if you'd rather go out, we can do that too."

"No. If you don't mind, I'd rather not go out. Besides, I don't have anything to wear. I hope you don't mind about your shirt. Mine was covered in blood."

"No, I don't mind. In fact, wear whatever you want of mine. I love seeing you in my shirt all tousled like this." He pulled his chair back from his desk and patted his lap. When she was seated in his arms, he continued. "Are you really okay?"

"Yes. I'm sorry. I've probably ruined the mood for you, huh?" She leaned back against him and looked around the room.

It was a beautiful study/office. She could see herself working in a room like this. The walls were covered in shelves and most of them were filled with books. And pictures—of the family she had met and some of them she had not. She looked at the picture of the older man with Devin's mother and recognized Devin in the man. She leaned forward and picked it up.

"It's my grandfather. This was his house. He let me buy it from him before he died. He let each of us buy one thing that he treasured most. I got this house, Spencer got his car, let's see, Byron got his art, and Nicky bought the Grant building from him. Damon bought his home in France. And Jamie bought his boat. They were things he treasured because he said he had spent time with our grandmother with these things and wanted us to earn them. He always made us earn everything, including our educations. I miss the old buzzard."

"I take it he was your father's father. You look a great deal like him. What were their names?" She set the picture back down on the shelf and looked at him.

"My grandmother was Elizabeth Marie Damon Grant and my grandfather was Spencer James Devin Grant. Devin was his mother's maiden name and he was named for her and then me for him. My mother said I even act like him too. He was a doctor of law. And a Circuit Judge. He died five years ago, just after my grandmother. It hurt them both badly when my dad died. Gramps always said a man should never outlive his child."

"So who are Byron and Nickolas named for?" Ronnie got up to take a closer look at the pictures now that she had some history.

"Smart girl. My father is named for Gram's side of the family. Her mother's maiden name is Nickolas and my dad's middle name —only the one—is Byron. Nickolas Byron Grant. Come here, Veronica."

She looked at him over her shoulder and shivered. His eyes had darkened again and she felt the heat from across the room. When she didn't move, he stood and moved toward her. Watching him walk was like seeing what sex looked like if it moved.

His body was hard and strong. She wanted to lean into him and never pull away. The closer he got to her, the stronger her pulse picked up, and she could feel her body reacting to his. When he ran his finger slowly down her arm, she could feel the heat of his touch through his sleeve she had on.

"You asked me if you ruined the mood and I wanted to tell you that you didn't. You only changed it. I want you more now than I did before. You have endured so much and I can't believe my luck to have you here with me."

"You still want me? After all of that, you still want to have sex with me?" She knew that she sounded surprised by his declaration, but she had fully expected him to turn her out.

"No, baby, I never wanted to have sex with you. I want to make love with you and to you. I want to feel your body under mine. I want to taste you and make you mine. I'm in love with you, Veronica."

She didn't know what she had expected him to say, but that was not it. He loved her? How was that even…

"You don't need to say that to have me stay with you, Devin. I want to be here with you."

He picked her up in his arms and sat down with her across his lap in one of the wingchairs by the window. Then he adjusted her around so that she was straddling his hips, much like she had been when he had made her come in his car. Only this time, she was nearly naked. She tried to pull his shirt down to cover herself and he stilled her hands.

"I love you, you stubborn woman. I love you with all my heart. I want you right now, in an hour, and will probably in the morning too. But I do want you. But if at any time you want me to stop, I will, and I won't hurt you. I won't make you feel bad for it. All right?"

She nodded and leaned in to kiss him.

~~~

Devin held himself back from the kiss. He didn't want to frighten her or make her feel like he was going to hurt her. He had spent the better part of the last three hours on the phone with first Damon then Morgan.

Morgan had been raped and sent to prison for killing the man who had done it to her. Randall, the rapist, had kidnapped her from her home and had tied her to a bed in his basement. He had done unspeakable things to her, raping her with not only his body, but with whatever he could find to use on her. He had also sold her to his friends when they came by. When the police had come to arrest him, Randall had gone to get a gun to kill her then probably himself. Morgan had broken her hand several times by bashing it against the wall and the headboard of the bed to pull her hand free of the handcuff. When he came through the door, she overpowered him and killed him with his own gun. Had not the police gotten there a few minutes later, she would have turned the gun on herself and had, in fact, had the gun pointed there to do so when a young rookie shot her in the arm to stop her.

"You have to let her talk about it. No matter how hard it is to hear, she needs to get it out," Morgan told him.

Devin did not tell her the details, but had hinted enough of them to let her know that he was worried about Ronnie. She had also advised him to have sex the first time in a bed. It would make her feel like he cared about her and not the act itself. With that in mind, he picked her up and carried her to his bedroom, the one she had been asleep in.

Laying her down on the mattress, he stood over her and, when she looked panicky, he kneeled down on the bed and smiled at her. He sat on his heels between her legs. His cock was protesting the tightening of his groin area, but he mentally promised it that it would be well worth the wait and a little discomfort.

Without taking his eyes from hers, he ran his hands up her calves then her thighs. Her skin was warm and smooth. Then he remembered something Damon had said. "Tell her everything you're going to do to her."

"I love to touch you. Your skin is warm and soft. I love the feel of your muscles bunching up when I touch you. Relax, honey, I'm not going to hurt you."

"I thought your hands would be smooth, but their callused and hard. You have the most incredibly long fingers I've ever seen on a man." He noticed that her voice was husky and soft, but her eyes gave away her emotions. They were dark with desire.

"I help build homes for the poor with Jamie in the spring and summer. I love being outdoors." He moved up her body until he was just between her knees. Leaning forward, he stretched out his arms and moved his shirt up her body to expose her panties. They were bright pink. He smiled.

"Are these the pair you had on the day I asked you what you had on? I nearly came in my trousers when you told me what you were wearing. I thought I was going to have to go to the bathroom and make myself come to the image of you in a pair of pink underwear."

"Devin...please?" He moved his hands further up her body until he found her navel. It was pierced. Devin moaned when he saw the tiny ring and leaned forward, licked the indented area, and laved the ring with his tongue.

His cock was aching to be released and as much as he wanted to free himself, he somehow knew that she was not ready for him. This had to be about her and he was damned well going to give her as much pleasure as she could take— even if he nearly killed himself doing it.

Kissing his way up her ribs, he nipped and touched every part of her he exposed. He could taste her heat, sweet and spicy. The fine sheen of sweat covering her even tasted delicious on his tongue. When the shirt bunched under her breasts, he moved up her body again. This time, he pressed his weight on top of her. Slowly, gently, he lifted the shirt until her bra was the only thing in his way of the most luscious bounty he had ever seen.

"Help me get this shirt off, baby. I want to see you." He could never remember his voice sounding so dark and rich. Nor his need to please so great.

His cock hardened even more when she lifted her head and he pulled the shirt up and over her. She lifted her hands and started to cover her; he stilled her with his larger ones.

"No. Don't. I want to look at you. Unsnap it for me. I want to watch as they spill from their confines and fill my hands."

With trembling hands, she moved to the small clasp and with a snap, the tiny scrap of lace covered but did not hold.

Moving his thumbs up beneath them, he rubbed her hard nipples and moaned. They were larger than he remembered; her nipples were an inch long, hard and erect and as thick as this thumb. Flipping his fingers up, he freed them with a small bounce.

"Christ, you're beautiful." Leaning down, he took the first one into his mouth and suckled just on the tip. Her legs moved up his body and wrapped around his hips. He surged into her heat before he could think to stop. Her answering groan had him press again. When she wrapped her hand into his hair and arched into his mouth, he opened over her breast and laved as much as he could with his tongue. Over and over he suckled and licked her; her body was riding his and it was all he could do not to throw back his head and howl with pleasure.

"Devin, please, I want to feel your skin next to mine. I want to touch you, touch you like you are me."

For as much has he did not want to leave her breasts, he wanted to give her what she wanted. And if she wanted him naked, then who was he to refuse her? He stood up and nearly fell back on her when he looked at the lust in her eyes.

"Show me. Take off your pants. Show me your cock. Now, Devin. Take them off now." He had no idea where she had gotten this streak of boldness, but he didn't care.

His hands went to his waistband before she finished his name. His shirt was next. It joined the growing pile of clothing that was now spread over the room. When he turned back to her after pulling it off, his own groan rippled from his throat. Before him lay a goddess and she was all his.

Devin's cock was hard. As thick as her wrist and long, he knew that he was very well endowed and fleetingly wondered if he would fit into her, then didn't care. He just would. Need, lust, desire for her all fought for control of him.

When he started walking toward her, he fisted his cock and began sliding up and down his shaft. A drop of pre-cum at the tip was now a stream of the pearly white substance. Hunger for her coiled in his belly and made him dizzy with desire.

"Veronica, I really want to feel your luscious mouth on my cock. Please, baby, even if you just slide your hot tongue over me, I'll probably come."

Reaching out when he was close enough for her to touch, she wrapped her hand around him and he jerked forward with a hiss. Her hand was hot and it seared into his flesh like a touch from the sun.

When she took a tentative lick at the bulbous dark head, he closed his eyes at the wondrous feel of her. Deep, dark and hot thoughts rumbled in his mind, things he wanted to do to her, with her, and her to him. But not now, not when she needed him. When he pulled back from her, she whimpered, and then started to sit up.

"I have no experience with...men. I...I was overwhelmed with need. No, that's not true, I was overwhelmed period. I didn't mean to hurt you."

"Hurt me? Christ, it's everything I can do not to pounce on you right now. You didn't hurt me, quite the contrary. But had you have taken me into your mouth again, I would have come—hard and fast deep into your throat."

"Okay." It was the smile, he decided. It said to him, bring it on and do your worst.

"Veronica, take off your panties." His voice was demanding, but she didn't seem to mind. He moved closer to the bed, dropped before her and nudged her legs further apart as he helped her move to the middle of the mattress. Her eyes were dark and hooded and when he touched his mouth to hers in a kiss, he felt the room spin.

"Please. Devin, please, I feel...needy. I don't know what to do, but I burn for you. Help me, please?"

"Open your legs honey. I'll help you. I'm going to help us both. Christ, you're so wet. I'm going to taste you, lick you until you come." He sounded as urgent as she looked.

When his finger brushed over her mounds, she cried out and arched up. She begged him to hurry because rather than help her, he was making it worse, for both of them. He slid his finger in then out of her, over and over until she began to sob for him to please help. He thought about his cock sliding into her wet heat and nearly sobbed himself. Leaning down, he closed his mouth over her clit and he nipped at her until she screamed out her release, crying out his name. He grabbed his cock and fisted it once, then again and came with her, spilling his seed all over his hand and the floor as he continued to lick and fuck her with his mouth and tongue.

~*Chapter 14*~

Ronnie woke to a semi-dark room, the light from a bathroom spilling across the floor in a long strip. For several seconds, she didn't know where she was and the arm around her waist frightened her more than she would have believed. When she realized it was Devin and she was in his bed, she relaxed back against the pillow.

She was in bed with Devin Grant! Just a few weeks ago, she would never have thought of being here, much less naked. Moving her leg slightly, she realized that he had on a pair of underwear, and she also realized that his cock was hard. An overwhelming need to giggle had her pulling the corner of the pillow over her mouth. She rolled over and tried to get out of bed, just realizing that she needed to go to the bathroom.

"Lie still. Damn it, woman, you always this squirmy when you wake up? We will have to do something about that if you are." He rolled over and tried to tuck her back under his arm.

"I have to pee. Let me up or I'll have an accident right here. And why should you care how I wake up?" She nearly

129

burst out laughing when he jumped up, but sobered quickly when she looked at him.

She had already known that Devin was handsome. His face looked to be carved from solid rock, but looking at his nearly nude body again, she was sure that no other man or stone could come close to the perfection that she had before her.

His face had stubble over his jaw and gave him a very bad-boy look. His shoulders looked as wide on one side as her whole body was and he had two of them. His chest, covered in a fine, dark fur across his nipples and narrowed as it went down to his waist, looked powerful and delicious. The narrow strip of hair disappeared into the top of his dark blue jockey's. The tribal around his arm was wide and looked to be about two inches in width. The lines of dark ink curving and twined into a very intricate design that seemed to play into his bad-boy image, but not the conservative lawyer one. His thighs were muscled and thick, his calves and shins also covered in the dark hair, and looked like he ran daily. When he groaned, she looked back up at his face.

"You keep looking at me like that, Veronica, and I'm going to have to take another cold shower. I can see the need in your eyes."

"Why did you take a cold shower?" She couldn't seem to get enough of looking at him. Her mouth felt dry, but her body did not.

"Because, love, I don't want to hurt you and I was going to sleep with you even if I had to take one every ten minutes. When I make love to you completely, it's going to be slow and easy."

She looked at his cock straining against the soft fabric and wondered what it would feel like to have him slide into her. Wondered what it would feel like to have him come inside of her. Ronnie blushed when she felt her wetness seep from her pussy.

"What if I don't want slow? What if...I want to feel you inside of me, Devin? I need to feel you touching me like you did before. I want you to make love to me, now."

She lay back on the bed and opened her legs. She felt wanton and shy, but the burning lust she saw in his eyes made her feel stronger. Running her hand down her breasts, she cupped them the way that he had and pinched her nipples. The same tingle she had gotten last night simmered in her belly.

"More. Squeeze them more for me. Make your nipples hard and achy for me." His voice poured over her and made her pussy feel heated; her blood felt hot as it raced along her veins.

She looked up at him as she twisted her nipple with her thumb and finger and moaned. Her legs widened more, as if they knew that something or someone was going to fill them. When Devin leaned against the post of the bed, she took her free hand and moved it over her navel and played with the small hoop there. His groan again made her want to please him more and she lowered her hand to her mound and slid one finger into her slit.

"Devin, I want you. I want to feel you fill me, bury your cock inside of me, please?"

"Show me your pussy, Veronica. Open for me so that I can see how wet you are. Show me that sweet pussy that tasted so delicious last night." He moved forward and took off his briefs. His cock was standing hard and straight from his groin and it was everything she could do not to leap up and pull him into her. When he sat on the edge of the bed with her, she whimpered. Taking her other hand, she opened for him and watched as he leaned in and swiped his tongue along the exposed flesh.

"Please, please, don't tease me. I need you." Her voice surprised her; it was dark and husky, demanding and hard. When he grinned at her, she wanted to bash him over the head.

Then he was moving over her. He settled between her thighs and his cock rubbed over her clit as he pressed against her. Cupping her breast, he pulled the hard nipple into his mouth and suckled. The pressure was building again. The need that he had brought her to was building quicker with him this close, him touching her.

"Baby, I don't want to hurt you, but you know it will, don't you? This first time it will hurt you when I break through your virginity. Do you want me to make it slow or fast for you? Fast will hurt more, but will be over quicker. I understand, but slow will kill me. But it's up to you."

"You've never taken a virgin before? I'm your first? I don't want you to die. What if I like this and you won't be around to do it again, then what? I'd have to find someone else to do this with." She didn't know why that made her feel special, but it did.

His growl made her giggle, but he did answer her. "No, you're my first. And after this, you will not be finding someone else to fill you. I'll beat your bottom if you even try."

He brought his mouth over hers. The kiss was savage almost, possessive and commanding. His tongue dueled with hers and touched deep into her mouth. She felt his cock then, nudging slightly at her entrance. He let go of her mouth, took her nipple in deep and suckled hard. Every nerve ending in her body exploded when he nipped her hard.

"Now! Take me now, Devin." And he did.

132

Pain caused her to cry out; it was immediate and hot. She wanted him to stop, to pull out, but could not form the words over the way her body was screaming at her. She could feel tears streaming down her face and buried her face in his shoulder. That was when she realized he was talking to her.

"I'm sorry, baby. I'm so sorry I hurt you. Just let me go, relax, sweetheart, and I'll pull out. Christ, he said it would only hurt for a second and then you'd be all right. Relax, baby. You have me so tight I don't dare move."

"Who said it would only hurt for a second?" She tried relaxing. She started at her toes and began to work her up her body, telling each muscle to relax and then move on. It worked when she was overly tired.

"Damon. I called him and...baby, don't do that. When you move like...yes, like that. I...that feels so good. Stop it!" His voice was strained and she found she liked that.

"You called Damon to ask him how to have sex with a virgin? And just how many virgins has he deflowered? And I like moving like this. It feels good." She surged up harder this time and felt him bite gently into her shoulder. For some odd reason, that felt as good as him moving into her now.

"I don't know, it seemed like a...do you think we can not talk about Damon right now? Do you still hurt? I can stop now. Well, maybe if you would stop moving like that. Veronica, you're killing me, baby. I don't want to...baby!"

She wrapped her legs around his hips and her arms around his shoulders. He felt good there, snug against her, inside of her. She tried to relax her pussy a little and he growled. She did it again and he bit her again.

When he moved inside of her, she moaned. Wrapping tighter around him, she moved up when he rocked into her. Soon they had a rhythm going and she felt the pressure building again. His mouth and his hands were everywhere, touching and caressing her, nipping and licking her. She was going up in flames and he was coming with her.

"Come for me, baby. I want to feel you come over my cock. Please, baby, come now." Her body responded to his command like a switch being turned on. Arching up and into him, she came apart.

Over and over her body surged, heat screamed along her legs and arms as she came. As soon as she began to come down, he would rock into her again and bring another climax to peak — twice, three times, she came. When he stiffened over her and rocked into her hard and tight, she felt him come, felt the hot cum splash against her womb, and she came again, screaming out his name.

He dropped over her and she slipped into a sated darkness.

~~~

When Devin opened his eyes, the room was filled with light. He picked up his cell phone and was shocked at the time. It was nearly noon; he never slept this late. Reaching beside him, he found an empty pillow and a cold space. Damn it all to hell, she had left him. He sat up, wondering how to contact her when he sniffed. Coffee.

Pulling on a pair of sweat pants, he ran down to the kitchen and stopped just inside the door. She was standing at the stove in one of his shirts again. Her laptop was sitting on the table and he could just make out some word document on it.

He watched as she put a slice of bread into some sort of batter in a bowl then placed it in the pan. She repeated this twice more until the pan was full. Seemingly satisfied with that, she picked up a fork and turned over some bacon. The smells alone had him salivating; the woman had him rock hard. When she turned toward the computer again, she saw him.

"I didn't hear you. I made something to eat. I was really hungry and I thought that I'd make us something. You don't have a lot of staples in your pantry, did you know that? It doesn't matter, I guess, since you probably eat out a lot. I hate to eat out. I don't like to eat alone either, but—"

"Veronica, you're babbling. Slow down and tell me what's wrong. Is it because we didn't use protection? I'm really sorry about that. I want you to know that I'm clean; you won't have to worry about that." He reached into the cabinet over the coffee pot and pulled down a mug and poured him a cup. It was hot and strong, just the way he loved it. He leaned against the counter where she was and waited. It didn't take her long.

"I'm on the pill so you know that I'm clean too. I have problems with...when I...Devin, I don't know what this means. I mean, we had sex and it was good, really good, but now what? I don't want you to declare your undying love or anything, but do we date now? Do we go our separate ways? It was really good, but I don't have a great deal to compare it to. Not that I want to. I sincerely doubt there would be any comparison actually. Make yourself a plate."

It took him a full five seconds before he caught onto the plate reference and then only because she jammed the plate into his chest. He took it and she put several slices of French toast on it, then poured warmed syrup over it. She was putting on the eighth slice of bacon before he grabbed her hand to stop her. He waited until she sat with her own plate before he answered her.

"Okay, first, and most importantly, I do love you. I think I have from the moment you called me a jackass. Secondly, you most certainly are not going to go comparing me to other men. You and I are together as of right now. Dating? Oh yeah, we're going to date, but we are also going to have sex, lots and lots and lots of it—every day, everywhere, in every position. Chew, baby, before you choke. And if you would, I'd very much like for you to move in here with me. As soon as possible—like today."

She chewed her bite and he could see the questions churning in her eyes—also a touch of anger. He smiled at her. She was never going to let things get too dull, that was for sure.

"I most certainly am not moving in here with you. I have a place to live. We don't even get along most of the time. Can you imagine how much we would be fighting if we lived together? And your mom, she doesn't strike me as the 'they're grown men; let them live their own lives' kind of mom. What is she going to say about this arrangement you're thinking about?"

"She'll snatch me bald then probably console you about having to put up with me. We get along just fine. And, besides, making up is a lot of fun. Why, I might even pick a fight with you just to make up with you. I guess that only leaves one way to settle this." He picked up his last slice of bacon, bit it in two, and smiled at her as he chewed.

He watched her eyes glitter with anger. He knew that if he did not explain soon, he would be wearing her plate, along with whatever she had left in her juice glass, very soon. Standing, he put his plate in the sink, took hers from her, and deposited it there as well. When she stood up, he pulled her into his arms and kissed her.

She tasted of the sweet powdered sugar she had sprinkled on her toast and the slight bitter tang of the orange juice. She smelled of maple and butter, warm and fresh. Her body was warm and soft, and when her arms came up around his neck, he cupped her ass and lifted her up. Her legs wrapped around his hips and he turned and sat her on the counter. Pulling away slightly, he cupped her face with his hands and looked deeply into her eyes.

"I do love you, do you know that? You are the best thing that has ever happened to me and I'm not going to let you go. Veronica Frey, will you marry me so that my mom won't kill me? Will you marry me so that I can fight with you and then have make up sex with you every night? Will you marry me because I love you, and will love you until the end of time?"

"Oh, Devin, you jackass." He burst out laughing. Not the answer he was hoping for, but one that he should have expected from her.

"Is that a yes? Because it doesn't really warm me up like I was hoping it would. I know that we've not known one another very long, but my heart knows that you're the one for me. If you need time to think about it, I can give you that. Will five minutes be enough?"

She smacked him across the shoulder and he moved in closer again. He loved touching her and when she leaned back against the cabinet behind her and pulled him with her, he took full advantage of her exposed throat. He was just making his way down her collarbone when the phone rang. He decided to ignore it when his mother's voice demanded his full attention from the answering machine.

"Devin Kyle Grant, why aren't you here? And you had better not be having sex with that poor girl. She is supposed to be convalescing, not cavorting." He snatched up the phone before her temper continued to boil.

"Mom? What a pleasant surprise. And yes, I did have sex with Veronica and now she won't make an honest man of me and say yes. I tried to stop her, but she was a mad woman, tearing at my clothes and my poor body." Ronnie started beating on his chest as her face turned several shades of red; his mother just sputtered. He had never had so much fun before. When his mom asked to speak to Ronnie, he had to nearly hold her down to make her take the phone.

"I didn't do anything to him, Mrs. Parker. He did...yes, ma'am he did...Yes, ma'am I'm sure you're right... Oh, I agree with that one. He can be the biggest jackass ever born...Today? I don't think...Yes, ma'am." Ronnie handed him back the phone and slipped off the counter. He put the phone to his ear.

"Mom? What did you do to her?" He had noticed the tears in Ronnie's eyes when she walked away and he was not having it, mother or no mother.

"You and she are coming here for dinner. I'll expect you within the next two hours so no fooling around. I mean it Devin. I'll snatch you balder than your Uncle Phillip if you don't get here on time. The rest of your family is here and I won't tell them that you've proposed. Did you have a ring? If not, you'll use the one your grandfather gave your grandmother. Nicky gave Morgan the set your father gave me. I'll see you in two hours." Then she hung up. He replaced the receiver in the cradle and went to find Ronnie.

~*Chapter 14*~

They had to make a trip to the mall. Ronnie didn't have any clothes and it was quicker to go by the mall than her home. She was the fastest shopper he had ever been with. She went into one of the specialty shops, picked out three tops and two pairs of pants, and paid before he could even get out his credit card. When they went to the lingerie shop, he had his credit card out when she was finished, but decided that he would live longer if he put it away. He decided that her looks would rival his mom's any day.

They were on the road again in less than twenty minutes. She got into the back of his SUV when they got back to the car and he had been hard pressed to keep his eyes on the road and not try to watch her change in the back seat.

"Devin Grant, if we have an accident while I'm naked in the back seat I'm going to kick your ass, I swear. Keep your eyes straight ahead and I'll finish faster instead of trying to figure out ways to sit so that you don't get a peep show." Her voice was muffled and he watched as the shirt she had just bought came down over her head. He got a nice view of the little piece of lace she had just bought, as well, and had to adjust his cock again.

"But I want a peep show. Besides, I think if we had an accident while you were naked, the paramedics would thank me. I know I would if I were them." Her growl made him laugh.

"So it would be all right with you if perfect stranger ogled my body instead of helping me? That doesn't say a lot for my wellbeing now, does it? I'm almost finished. Damn it, I forgot socks. Do you think anyone will mind if I take my shoes off and my feet are bare?"

"No, I don't want anyone even thinking about looking at your body. You're right, get dressed. And for socks, I'm sure Mom will have a few pair around. Besides, nobody is going to be looking at your feet. You're much too beautiful for anyone to notice that you have feet."

When she slid between the seats and sat in the passenger seat and buckled in, he looked at what she had bought. She looked lovely. He smiled when he thought about Nicky.

Nicky had called him several weeks ago when he had had to go shopping with Morgan to get her dress for the dinner. He said that he had been with her for over six hours and he was bored out of his mind. He thought the first dress she had tried on was fine, but no, she had to try on fifty more just in case. In case what? he had yelled at Devin. He could not wait to rub it in.

"Devin, what is your mom going to say about you asking me to marry you? She didn't seem too happy with me when I talked to her. She scares me just a little."

He kissed her hand he had been holding since she'd sat down. "She told me to give you my grandmother's ring. I'm sorry I didn't have one for you when I asked you. I should have thought of that. But this will be better. It's a pretty ring. My grandfather gave it to my grandmother a few years after they were married. He couldn't afford the one he wanted to give her when they married, so he promised her he would buy her one when he made his first million. So that was the first thing he bought when he started investing and it paid off."

"But it's a family ring. I shouldn't have a family ring. What if it doesn't work out, or I lose it?" He didn't say anything. She didn't say she didn't want it, she said she didn't want to lose it. That was as good as a yes as far as he was concerned. They were pulling into the drive when she remembered her test.

"I can't stay tonight. I have my boards tomorrow morning. I forgot all about them. I'm sorry; you don't have to drive me back. I can take a cab or something. I have to...what is so funny?"

"I told you, love. You're mine and you aren't getting away from me. If you want to fight about me bringing you back in the city, that's fine with me. I'd much rather be home right now buried deep within you rather than at this family dinner. As much as I love my family, right now, I can't seem to get enough of you, and you're way more beautiful."

When they were on the front porch and just before he opened the door, he pulled her back into his arms and kissed her. She responded just like he had hoped she would. She settled in close to him and pulled him tighter. Her mouth opened under his and before he knew it, he had her pressed hard against the wall of the house and was cupping her ass to bring her closer to his erection. The door opening beside them was probably the only thing that saved them from letting the entire neighborhood watch them have sex against the wall.

"Mom said to tell you to quit groping her and both of you get inside before Mrs. Andrews across the street calls the police. From the blush that Dan had when she looked at him, I'm assuming we don't want to know why she knows this.

Hello, Ronnie. Your shirt's buttoned wrong." Spencer smiled at him and winked at Ronnie. Her face was a bright red when they went inside.

Dinner at his mom's was a weekly thing. They had been doing it since the first one of the boys had moved out and they looked forward to it mostly for the getting together more than the food. Thankfully, his mom did not cook.

This week's dinner was beef roast and browned potatoes with gravy, green beans and peas. There were hot dinner rolls and warm cornbread. For desert there was fresh baked apple pie with ice cream. They were nearly ready to sit down when Mrs. Poole, the woman who had been cooking for the family since Devin was a baby, dropped the gravy boat and spilled the gravy.

Damon tended to her slight burns while everyone finished up decanting the dinner. Mrs. Poole was beside herself because of the gravy not being there.

"It's Mr. Devin's favorite too. What with him bringing a girl home and all. And I had to go and ruin it for them. Such a lovely couple you both are too. I'm so sorry, miss."

"I can make gravy. I love to cook. It won't take a minute. That is, if you don't mind me using your kitchen. Devin has very few staples in his cabinets; it's a shame. I'm sure it won't be as good as yours, but I can try."

"You can cook too? Oh my, you have done well for yourself, haven't you, Mr. Devin? You go ahead, miss. Make him some. Never seen a boy like gravy like he does, you know."

Ronnie took some of the beef and fired it up in a pan to make some brown makings. Adding a little milk and water to some flour, she was whipping up some very smooth brown gravy in less than three minutes. Mrs. Poole approved and everyone insisted that she join them for their meal. It was a grand one too—lively conversations, children laughing and teasing between the families. Ronnie watched it all in awe. Devin leaned over and pulled her close to kiss her.

"You okay? I know we are a bit to take at first, but we sort of grow on you. My dad would take pictures and then show them off the following week. Dan has started taking pictures after dinner when we are all at our worst. I think there's an album around somewhere with a bunch of them in it."

"I'm fine. It's so different than when Austin, Ben and I eat. Even when their friends come over, it's fairly quiet and reserved. This...this is amazing. How do you keep up with each other's conversation?"

"It's impossible. But don't let that worry you, honey. You'll get used to us. Would you mind if I borrowed Devin for a few minutes, please? I promise I won't keep him long," Margaret said with a small pat to Ronnie's cheek.

Devin kissed Ronnie and went with his mother. They were headed to the study and he felt his stomach jump with anticipation. She was going to give him the ring and Ronnie had never said yes yet.

When she opened the safe and handed him the small jeweler's box, he took a deep breath. The last time he had looked at this ring was when he had been just out of law school and his grandmother had given it to him.

"This ring isn't the one he proposed to her with, of course. That ring is with Morgan. But I believe I love this ring more. He had gotten it for her on Valentine's Day and she cried, she told me. He had buried it in a piece of chocolate and he was so terrified that she would swallow it before he could see it on her finger."

Devin opened the box and marveled once again at the beauty of the setting. The diamond was blue, rare now, but even more so then. The band was an inch wide of twenty-four carat white gold. There was an inscription on the inside, the year that his grandfather had given it to his beautiful bride. The diamond was a full two carats and square cut held in place with a gold figurine design that swirled over the gem and along the band. There were no other gems with it; the simplicity of it was perfect for Veronica in that.

"It's perfect for her, Mom. Perfect. But, I'm nervous. I'm...she never told me yes when I asked her. I don't know what I'll do if she tells me no." He looked at her and she opened her arms to him. Even as old as he was, Devin loved hugging his mom almost as much as he loved receiving them from her.

"She'll say yes. How could she not? She is a pretty little thing, isn't she? All prim and proper. Are her parents nice?"

Devin laughed. He couldn't help it. "First, she's not so prim. I think we just overwhelmed her. About her parents, her father is Austin Pride, an artist that I guess Byron knows, and her mother is Ben Kendal. He designs dresses. That dress she wore to the dinner is one of his."

"Ben Kendal of Kendal's Boutiques—that Ben Kendal? Devin, do you have any idea who those men are? I think I have it here...just a minute." He watched as she went to the desk and pulled out several magazines and then came back at him with a Fortune 500. She had it open and handed him the glossy article.

There were both their names, Austin's in the first slot and Ben's the third one down. They were considered two of the three richest men in the world. He sat down hard on the chair that was thankfully right behind him. He skimmed through the article that described them both as reclusive men, yet donated millions of dollars to charities every year; their pet ones were mostly those that dealt with child abuse and the wellbeing and welfare of children. He smiled, wondering how long it had been a project of theirs, and wondered if the time coincided with the arrival of one Veronica Frey.

"You should call Austin and ask him for her hand. It's a nice thing to do. Plus, they should know that you asked her. I would want to know that you had if she were my daughter. You call; I'll go see what she's up to."

She was in the kitchen with Morgan and Mrs. Poole.

~~~

Ronnie was washing the dishes that wouldn't fit in the dishwasher and listening to the other women talk. She didn't have many friends and very few of them were women. She was surprised and pleased that Morgan was so friendly to her and her little boys were so adorable.

"How long did you know Mr. Grant before you guys got married?" Ronnie asked, and immediately felt bad when she saw the quick look of pain flitter across Morgan's face.

"We didn't exactly have the best of beginnings. Nick married me because I was pregnant with his twins and sort of fell in love with me afterwards. But it's all worked out. I love him very much and he loves me. Has Devin told you he loves you yet?"

"Yes, today as a matter of fact. He told his mother this afternoon when she called. I'm not sure what to think of all this. It's sort of sudden and we really haven't known each other all that long either. He, well, he asked me to marry him too."

The noise that came from Morgan had Ronnie go for her gun, but luckily, she was grabbed in a bear hug that prevented her from reaching it. Mrs. Parker came in while Ronnie was trying to disengage herself from Morgan.

"They're getting married! Isn't that wonderful? Another woman in the family to shop with, Margaret. Isn't that great? Oh, I'm so happy for you both."

"I just said he asked me. I didn't say I said yes. And to be honest, I'm not so sure I will. I mean, I don't exactly come from a normal background." Boy, that was an understatement.

"I've met your parents, Ronnie. Well, at least your father. He's a very eloquent man. I was impressed with the speech he gave at a luncheon I attended," Margaret told her with a smile.

"My father? I've never...mine? Are you sure? He can barely put two sentences together without making you want to bash him over the head. I remember once a teacher told him that he should maybe attend grade school. His grasp of the English language is horrendous."

"Darling, I'm talking about Austin Pride. Not that horrid man who sired you. And I understand that Ben Kendal is your...I'm sorry dear, is he your mother or another father? I want to be very correct in this when we get together to plan your wedding."

"Roommate. What do you mean, plan my wedding? I'm getting married? Listen, you guys need to take a deep breath and back off. I never said I was marrying anyone. My head hurts." She sat down in the chair and put her head between her knees. Things were going entirely too fast for her and she needed...damn it, she needed Devin. She was going to kick his ass. "Can you please tell me where Devin is? This all may be a moot point if I kill him in the next hour."

Ronnie was directed to the study where he was and with a short knock, she opened the door. He was sitting behind a huge desk talking on the phone. The room was lit only by the fireplace and a small lamp across the room. It was a beautiful room.

The desk was dark and though the lights were off, the dark green antique lamp on it was brass and glass. The entire wall behind him was leaded glass in the most unique design she had ever seen. Through it she could see the pool, covered now for the winter, and lots of trees. The wall with the fireplace was floor to ceiling shelves, all glass fronted with the same leaded design that was in the windows. The mantel was eight feet long and very wide. Ronnie could see several pieces of pottery and pictures in old and new frames all along it. Over the roaring fire was a painting of an older woman and man, the man from the photo on Devin's desk at his home. The woman, she assumed, was his grandmother. The wall that the door she had come through had hanging photos, again old and new but all of people. She knew at once they were pictures taken by Devin's father, the pictures he had told her about.

The last wall, the one across the fireplace, was covered in another glassed in shelf, this one filled with trophies and all other sundry. She started to step toward it when she heard Devin say her name.

"Veronica is right here now...no, I haven't, but from the look on her face I would say that's a no...Yes, I'm sure you're right...All right, I'll have her call you as soon as I talk to her. Good night, Ben, and thanks." He hung up the phone and stared at her.

He was such a handsome man. His eyes nearly glowed with the firelight dancing in them. His hair was mussed; much like it looked when she had woke up this morning and looked at him. He had been running his fingers through it like he did when he was frustrated, mostly at her. Devin stared back at her and she wondered what was going on in

147

his mind then thought she probably didn't want to know. He looked tired and a little anxious.

"Come here, love. I need to hold you for a minute. My family, they're treating you all right?"

"Yes, and for now, I'll stay here. You might thank me for the added distance in a minute. Why is your mother planning my wedding? And why are you talking to Ben?" His grin told her nothing.

"I have something for you. Would you come here so that I can give it to you?" He had ignored her, but she was not as easily distracted as he thought.

"I asked you a question, counselor. Why did you call Ben and why is your mother planning a wedding that I'm the bride in?"

"You were there when I told her I had asked you to marry me. She seems to think you'll say yes because you are a smart girl. I told her that she didn't know you like I did and that you barely tolerated me at most. As for Ben, I was talking to Austin first and he put Ben on when he told me that I could ask for your hand." He stood up now and walked toward her. Her body responded and not how she wanted it to, damn it. "Austin thinks I'm a great catch too."

She snorted. Not very ladylike, but they were all backing her in a corner and she didn't like it. She straightened when he was a few inches from her. She didn't know whether to hit him or to throw him to the floor and ravage him. It was a toss-up. But her body was telling her to throw him to the floor and have at him like a large Sunday buffet.

When he dropped down on one knee, she tried her best to stop the giggle that erupted from her mouth. He raised a brow at her, but said nothing as he took her hand in his.

"Don't do this, Devin. Please? You don't know me very well. What if I'm a crazy person bent on destroying everything you have? Or I howl at the moon once a month?"

"Do you? Never mind, I don't care. That and many others are things I want to learn about you. I'm in love with you, Veronica. I love you with all of my heart and if you won't say you'll marry me, I'll tell my mother on you. And I know that you're crazy, by the way." She watched as he took the ring from his pocket and slipped it over her finger just to the first knuckle.

"What about children? I mean, you want some, right? What if they're like him? What if they are evil like my father?" She was grasping at straws and they both knew it.

"I would hope that you'd want children, but it's all right if you don't. And they won't be like him. I swear to you, baby, that I love you and we can and will be great parents. Veronica, quit stalling. Will you marry me?" He slid the ring onto her finger and kissed it. Then he looked up at her again.

"You are so going to regret this. I just know it, but yes. I'll marry you." His loud whoop had her jump back and he picked her up and swung her around the room. Before he sat her on her feet, his entire family came rushing in the room. She had a feeling that they had been listening at the door.

~*Chapter 15*~

The ride back to the city was not long, but it was quiet. Devin glanced over at Ronnie and smiled. She was listening to her small recorder with her eyes closed. He was sure that she wasn't listening to music, but notes. When she suddenly turned to him, he glanced guiltily at the road.

"Devin, do you think you could pull over and just hold me for a minute? I'm out of my mind with worry and I just want you to hold me." He pulled over immediately and unbuckled.

Ronnie started to slide his way, but he held up his hand and got out of the car to go around to her side. Opening the door, he reached in and turned off the overhead light and then unbuckled her as well. She stared at him for all of ten seconds, then turned and buried her face into his neck. He gripped her and pulled her closer to him. Nothing had ever felt so good, so complete.

"You could have just held me. You didn't need to get out and come around. But I'm glad you did. You're so warm and I love the way you smell."

Devin moved his fingers through her hair and lifted her face to look at him. Her eyes were dark in the moonlit night

151

and he wanted to taste her, even as the cold air blasted him from behind. Lowering his head, he took her mouth.

Devin wanted to be gentle, wanted to savor her taste, but as soon as his lips touched hers, he groaned. Need rolled through him and he poured all he was into her. Deepening the kiss, he shifted so that he was between her legs and she instinctively wrapped her legs around his hips and dug her heel into his thighs. Cupping her ass, he brought her forward and lifted her against his erection. She shuddered hard against his mouth and he groaned again.

"Every time you touch me, I feel like I'm going up in flames. Will there ever be a time when that never happens? I want to have you inside of me right now, Devin." She was panting and he surged harder against her tender folds.

"We are still thirty minutes from home and if you keep tempting me like this, I'm going to take you right here along the side of the road like a horny teenager. Behave, woman. I can only...Christ!"

Ronnie's hand cupped his balls and she rolled them. He felt his climax building. Never had a woman made him feel like this, and he doubted one ever would again. He moved against her hand over and over until he knew he was not going to last.

Suddenly, she was lying back on the seat working at the zipper on her pants and pulling them off. He watched her, mesmerized while she sat up and pulled off her shoes, and then down again to shimmy out of her pants. His cock jerked hard in his own pants.

"Don't just stand there staring at me, hurry. Someone may come along, and if you're not inside of me before then, I'm going to my house and you're going to be sleeping alone in that big bed of yours."

Devin didn't need to be told twice. He helped her with her jeans and then slid between her legs, his fingers moving into her heat immediately. She was wet, hot and her clit was as hard as his cock. Using his free hand, he unbuttoned his own pants and hurriedly tore down his zipper. His cock leapt forward as if it knew that time was of the essence and that she was ready for him.

Moving his fingers from her, he rocked his cock deep and Ronnie wrapped her legs around him all in one smooth motion. His balls tightened up close to his body and he knew that he was not going to prolong this for much longer. The few cars going by couldn't see what he was doing, but if anyone stopped to see if he needed anything, they would get the sight of their life. Grabbing her by her hips, he pulled her forward to the edge of the seat to hold her there and pounded into her. The excitement of where they were and that they could get caught at any moment added fuel to his already overwhelmed body. Pulling her out of the car and trapping her body against the back door, he stilled, needing to regain some control over himself and the situation.

"Oh, Devin, please...I want to come. I need to come soon, please," she whispered near his ear, and then she nipped at his neck.

"Feed me, baby. Give me your breasts. I want to suckle them. I want to suck them hard." Her hand were trembling when she pulled her shirt over her head and she was cursing the clasp before she just pulled her bra up over her breasts and lifted them to his mouth.

Leaning her back across the car, he took the offered bounty into his mouth. She moaned deep when he took the tip and worried it with his tongue before rolling it hard. When he opened his mouth wider, taking in as much as he could, he lifted his left hand up and pinched her nipple on the

153

other breast. She arched under him and he felt the tingle of his climax rushing through his body. Devin lifted his head and kissed her, deep, hard, his tongue fucking her mouth as hard as his cock was her pussy.

"Come, baby. Come and take me with you. Now, Veronica, come now," Devin begged her.

There was a slight pause, less than a heartbeat, when she grabbed his shoulders and screamed out his name. Her channel grabbed at him, milked him hard and tight. For seconds he thought he was going to pass out from the way she held him, pulsing hard along his length. Then his own body released wholly and completely into her. Over and over his cock surged, emptying himself and filling her. His knees weakened and his heart pounded. Breathing hard, all he could do was lean over her and rest his head on her breast and thought that if he died right now, he would die one happy man.

He raised his head to look at Ronnie, to tell her how much he loved her. He wanted to tell her how it had felt to have her in his life, to tell her that he would never regret marrying her no matter what. But he couldn't. She was asleep, her body lax and sated under him.

He reluctantly pulled from her and settled her back in the car. Straightening his clothes, Devin knew that he should wake her. He should help her dress, but she looked so peaceful and knew that she needed to rest for tomorrow. He gently lifted her and turned her in the seat and laid it back to the prone position. She never stirred. Taking off his long coat, he was just covering her up with it when a sudden burst of red and blue lights flashed behind him. Ronnie started to move and he lifted his coat over her face so that the lights would not wake her.

"Good evening, Officer." Devin didn't move when the man came out of his cruiser and flashed his light at them. Devin stepped in front of the open door. "My fiancée is asleep. I was trying to make her more comfortable without waking her. I didn't want her to hurt herself and get up sore tomorrow. We still have a ways to go before I get us home."

Officer Sharp didn't say anything, but he did lower his beam so that it only illuminated Devin's legs and not the girl lying there. He did, however, move closer to the car and look in. Devin backed up to give him room, but he didn't leave the open door.

"Where you coming from, young man? This isn't the best place to have stopped, you know. You should have gone down to the next pull off. There's a rest stop there."

"My mother's house, Margaret and Dan Parker. I'm Devin Grant and this is Veronica Frey. I never thought about the rest stop. I...well to be honest, she just became my fiancée tonight and I'm really not thinking all that well. You're actually the first person I've said that to."

Devin knew that he was grinning like an idiot, but he just couldn't seem to help himself. Officer Sharp didn't say anything more, just motioned for him to close the door when he stepped back.

"You drive carefully, Mr. Grant. You have some precious cargo in there. I know Ronnie—she's a good girl. My wife and I miss her at the diner. Tell her Daniel and Caroline Sharp said congrats."

When the cop was in his car, Devin walked to his side of the car and got inside. He leaned his head on the steering wheel and took a deep breath. Yeah, being married to Veronica was never going to be a dull moment, he thought as he started his car.

~~~

The noise was going to drive her crazy. She rolled over and threw her arm out to grab a pillow to pull over her head and it was suddenly jerked from her grip. Sitting up quickly, she squeaked in alarm. She was naked. Naked it a bed she didn't know. Naked in a bed she didn't know with a person.

"You are really annoying when you wake up, anyone ever tell you that? Can't you just wake up like a normal person? You know, roll over, hit the snooze button, and snuggle under the covers — quietly — for a minute or two? Why do you have to squirm and wiggle?"

"Devin?" She looked around the bedroom. She had been in his room before, but there hadn't been a lot of time to look around. It was a really nice room and huge.

"You know, you have a very annoying habit of saying stuff like that too. Who else's bed would you be in this early in the morning? I brought you here last night after you seduced me into having sex with you along the side of the road. By the way, Daniel Sharp said to tell you hello and congratulations on your engagement. He and his wife miss you at the diner. Then I had carried you up here and put you to bed. You are very relaxed when you go to sleep, aren't you?"

"Wait! Daniel Sharp? Officer Daniel Sharp? When did you see...oh my God! He didn't see us, did he? Oh, Devin, the things he must...he saw me... Oh, please kill me now."

"He didn't see anything. I was wrapping you in my coat when he pulled up. He saw who you were and I told him we had just gotten engaged and he said to tell you hi. Nothing more."

Ronnie peeked up at Devin from the pillow she had buried her face in. Then she glanced over at the clock. "Shit! It's seven o'clock. I have to be downtown in the court house at eight-thirty. Can you call be a cab while I shower?"

Ronnie didn't wait for him to answer, but shot out of bed and into his bathroom. She smiled when she heard him groan and then she saw herself in the mirror. She looked different — beautiful really.

Her skin glowed. It looked soft and warm, not that she had hard skin, but she thought it looked like she had rubbed it down with expensive lotions every day. Her hair was a mess, but it looked fuller and shinier. Her lips were swollen and that gave them a fuller pouty look. Her cheeks were red from Devin's whiskers and there were tiny bite marks over her breast and belly. She looked like a woman who had been well used and sated.

When she got into the shower, she realized that she was sore, sore in places she had never hurt before, especially between her thighs. Her face flushed more when she remembered how they'd gotten that sore and smiled. She was dressed and downstairs ten minutes after she hopped out of bed, braiding her hair as she stuffed her feet into her shoes. Devin was leaning against the counter drinking a cup of coffee with no shirt or shoes on. He looked good enough to eat.

"Take the SUV. I don't know what the weather is going to be like for the rest of the day, but it's snowing now. I have to go to the office this morning, but I can meet you for lunch if you want."

"I can't take your car. I don't want to wreck it, and I don't know what time I'll get lunch. The letter said I would take parts of the test and when they were finished, I would be given breaks between."

"Take the car, Veronica. And before you argue with me again, you should know that if I have to take you in, you'll be late. I have to be out of town tonight. I have to go take a statement in Akron State Pen, so do you want to come here, or will you go back to your house?"

Ronnie glanced at the clock then glared at him. "I'll stay at my house tonight. I want to see Austin and Ben. You really irritate me when you try to manipulate me. You know that, don't you?"

"Yes. But I don't care as long as you're safe. I'll call you tonight and see how things went. I should be back tomorrow evening, and then we'll have dinner. I love you. Now go, and be careful." He swatted her ass as she stalked past him. He was so going to pay for this.

The whole day was a blur of tests and questions. She had worked really hard to get to this point in her career and hoped that she didn't fail now. Ronnie knew that she could take the bar again, but she really wanted to get it finished. Judge Stone had told her she was the most brilliant lawyer he had ever met and was going to take her on as a junior partner when he retired. She was so sad when he had died.

Offers were coming to the house almost every day now. Sometimes as many as a dozen or more. She had a few set aside; the rest she had put into a folder to keep, just in case. She didn't know where she was going yet, but she knew the first thing she was going to do was take a long, much needed vacation.

When she got home after six, she was so excited to see Ben and Austin that she couldn't contain herself. They ordered Chinese and sat around the dining room table and talked for over three hours. And the package and the three dozen red roses from Devin made her entire night. She kept staring at them the whole evening.

The roses were sitting in her room on her dresser now, as she had carried them to her room when she had come up to bed, and she pulled out the cell phone Devin had sent her. She smiled at his note.

"You are going to have to pay for your own phones if you break this one. Do not let someone hit you with it, please. I've had it programmed. I love you. Devin"

She was just crawling into bed when he called her. "Hello, love. Have a good day?"

"Yes. Thank you for the phone. And I love the car. It handles so nice in the snow I may never give it back to you. And I can listen to my music without a set of headphones attached to my head to hear. Plus, the added bonus is that it smells like you, and sex." She giggled when he groaned.

"You are cruel. I'll be home tomorrow around two. I have an appointment with someone, a new client, and then you and I will meet for dinner. My mother called me a few minutes ago. She wants to know if you and Ben can meet her for lunch after your test. I think she's calling Ben now. Hummm, she wants to know if we can get married on Christmas. She said that Ben assured her your dress would be done by then."

Ronnie knew that Ben wanted to design her dress for her and that he and Austin were going to pay for the entire thing—as her parents, they felt it was their honor. Ronnie felt tears well again when she thought about them.

"I guess. I don't really care for Christmas, but maybe by next year I'll have a better frame of mind for it. If that's what you want anyway." He was so quiet that she was worried. "Devin?"

"I think they mean this Christmas. As in, six days from now. Mom said that she has that dinner thing every year anyway and it would be easy to have everyone go to the church first, and Ben said that their employees would love a reason to have a party. I know its fast, but I kind of like the idea of it being this Christmas. It means you're mine faster."

She didn't know what to say. Wasn't even sure she could say anything. Six days? Six days to plan and execute a wedding? Her nerves jumped. She didn't need any more pressure right now. Her belly churned even as she pressed her hand against it.

"Can we talk about this tomorrow? I'm...after my boards. Right now, I don't think I'd say yes to you again if you asked me to marry you. All right?"

"Of course, baby. I understand. You'd better go to sleep, and I'll talk to you tomorrow. I love you."

Ronnie thought she would toss and turn, but as soon as her head touched the pillow, she was out. And she didn't dream of her father, but of the man she loved very much.

Ronnie was finished with her test at two-ten the next afternoon. She called Ben and told him she could meet Mrs. Parker and him at Rugby's—a trendy restaurant downtown—and then texted Devin. She didn't want to talk to him while he was in his meeting. At two-thirty, she was sitting in the restaurant and had just ordered when her phone rang.

"Ronnie, it's your boss, Devin Grant. I've been trying to reach you. I've been wanting to..."

"He wants you to know that your daddy is back, and it's high time for us to get reacquainted."

~*Chapter 16*~

Devin hurt. The man who had made the appointment with him had pistol whipped him for the past hour trying to get information out of him about Veronica. Devin could feel his broken ribs and he was also sure his wrist was as well.

But it was not until he had threatened to kill Caroline that he had finally told him about the phone. But it had done Devin little good. Albert Frey had killed poor Caroline anyway. Now she lay dead on the floor next to him with a single gunshot wound to the temple. He had shot her because Veronica had not answered the phone the first time Devin had tried.

"You'll meet me at the old house in two hours or I kill this boss man of yours. And you'll come alone and not be late, Catalina. And if you tell anyone, you both die. Do I make myself clear, bitch?"

Devin wanted to scream at her not to come, that he was going to kill Devin anyway, but he could no nothing more than groan at the gag that Frey had returned to his mouth after he took the phone back.

"She'll come. She knows better than to defy me again. I'm as near her daddy as she'll ever get. She tried it once and I'll not let her get by with that again. Stupid cunt. And I was willing to break her into the saddle even knowing how fucking ugly she was. Ungrateful, that's what she is, ungrateful. Well, she's gonna pay now, by damn. Gonna pay big time. I'm gonna get her with child so I can have it to break in too. Yes, sir, gotta keep it in the family if you want it done right."

Devin thought he was going to be sick. This man acted as if having sex with his children was his responsibility, not a sick, twisted from of child abuse. Small wonder Veronica ran away. Devin's heart hurt for the little girl she had been and he knew he had to figure out some way to protect her. Even if it cost him his own life.

The appointment had been set up to help Mr. Albert finalize some paper work for his children. He had seemed sane, normal even. And when Devin had given Mr. Albert all he could in information concerning the situation, Devin stood and offered the man his hand. He had taken Devin's hand, telling him goodbye, then slipped a cuff over his wrist. At the moment the lock clicked into place, Frey had backhanded Devin across the face with his hand. Before Devin could react, both his hands were cuffed behind him and he was down on the floor bleeding from his lip and tongue where he had bitten it.

After Frey got off the phone with Veronica, he started pacing the room, even walking through Caroline's blood as if she was nothing, not even a stain on the rug. Devin wanted to talk to Veronica. He wanted to tell her how much he loved her one more time before he died.

"You know that morning if'n I hadn't come back for my hat, she'd be dead now? Stupid girl tried to off herself instead of just giving into me—when she knew damn good and well that I always get what I want. Didn't even know she knew there was a gun in the house. But she always was too big for her britches, always snooping around instead of keeping the house up like she should have been. Yeap, I was gonna use the toilet and there she was, a pointing that big old thirty-eight of my pappy's to her head. Thought she was shooting me at first when it went off. That's what made me so mad at her. Nerve of her! I'ma thinking, no way, she can't be trying and shoot her own daddy. Then I seed that I'd bumped her like and the bullet only grazed her." Albert paced some more.

"Still, had to teach her a lesson, didn't I? Gotta say, though, it's a good thing my sweet Margo comed in when she did. Hell of a mess, hell of a mess. Blood everywhere even though she had put down them towels. Still made a mess. Took me near an hour to clean it up too. Couldn't even count on her momma to help, the bitch, her laying up there all pickled like she always was. I can tell you I was none too happy about that either. Then I had to throw all them towels out too. Stupid girl. But I beat her too hard and weren't no way them nosey doctors was gonna believe that she fell this time. No siree. Had to come up with a plan, I did. Margo comed up with the robbery and Holly, the other precious light of my life, God rest her soul, said it would make people think she was a hero and if she got anything for it, they'd keep it because she wouldn't know what to do with pretty things. Smart girls, those two. But they had it right. Catalina weren't pretty like them."

Devin gagged on the rag in his mouth. Frey had beaten his little girl nearly to death because rather than subject herself to having sex with her father, she tried to kill herself. Catalina, Devin's Veronica, had preferred death over him. No wonder Veronica was afraid to trust people. She had not been able to trust the one man above all others who should have been there for her.

When Devin had told him about the cell phone, it took him nearly twenty minutes to explain to Frey what his "Catalina" needed one of them portable phones for. Devin had not told Frey that he was in love with Ronnie. He was reasonably sure that the man would hurt her worse for the knowledge. When Ronnie had answered the cell, Devin was both relieved and terrified for her.

It was nearly an hour later when Devin and Frey were headed out of the building, taking the elevator down to the basement garage to where Devin had parked his car. He wasn't sure what was going to happen once they got there, but he was sure it was not going to end well for him. Devin had been around enough criminals to know you did not give away the ending of the story to someone without thinking their victims were not going to be around to tell it to someone else. This had the "talking gunman syndrome" written all over it.

He heard the sirens as soon as they stepped out of the elevator. He hoped that Frey thought they were normal sounds of the big city and not for him. Devin's hopes for getting out of this alive were dashed as soon as they got to the car. After another hard blow to the head, Frey explained what his plans were for both him and Veronica.

"You're gonna die, you know that, don'tcha? Can't leave around no witnesses to this. I got me some babies to make. Now that I seen what a pretty little thing Catalina turned out to be, well, it won't be so hard for me to fuck her. Yeah, that was right nice of that photographer to put her pitcher in the paper. It was a nice one of her all dressed up in that dress. Called her Veronica Frey. But I knowed she was my little girl Catalina. Can't mistake those eyes. Bruises is what they always reminded me of—she sure had enough of them to compare them to." Frey actually chuckled at his own sick joke. "But you've been real helpful, I gotta tell ya. Well, buddy, you're gonna drive me to the house, then I'ma gonna kill you dead. Yep, can't leave no witnesses."

Devin started the little car he had driven to work today wondering if he could crash it. His luck, all he would do is kill himself and Veronica would still be raped. When he reached to put his buckle on, he dialed his cell phone. He didn't know who he had called, but figured any of the numbers he had programmed in the thing would be better than dying alone.

~~~

Ronnie walked out of the restaurant and hailed a cab. She was numb. Her father had Devin and she knew he would hurt him, if he hadn't already. Knowing this, knowing what her father was capable of, made Ronnie wish she had had better aim all those years ago.

Ronnie would never be sure how Ben had figured it out. But as soon as Ronnie heard her father's voice, she became six again and he was standing over her with his fist doubled up. She thought she had whimpered, but wasn't sure. Only now could she remember what her father had said to her. Just the sound of his voice made everything around her feel tainted and dirty, like he had sucked the very life out of all that he touched or saw.

Ronnie was to go to their old house in Nashport and meet him there. Devin, hopefully, would be with him and alive. And she only had two hours to get there. She would be lucky if she made it, but she would die trying. She had to save the man she loved.

Mrs. Parker seemed as solid as a rock. She and Ben planned and told her things would be all right, that she and Devin would both be fine. Ronnie wasn't so sure. She knew firsthand what sort of man her father was and he was not reasonable. Ronnie wasn't even sure if he had ever been sane, and wondered if he had just gotten crazier over the years.

"Devin won't die. I won't allow it and you won't either, do you hear me? You go there and kill this bastard and come back to us," Ben had said as he hugged her to him.

Ronnie could hear him make some phone calls, but she wasn't sure of all of them. Ronnie knew Ben had called the police and then Austin, but that was about all. Captain Tucker of the Columbus Police Force had also been informed. All Ronnie could think was, if Nickolas Grant didn't hate her before, he would now for sure.

"You'll need money. Take a cab. It'll be safer than you driving right now. Give me the address and we'll have someone there to rescue you both in the light of something going wrong." Ronnie started to cry. It was going to go wrong. It had already gone so very wrong.

Margaret took all the money she had in her wallet and stuffed it into Ronnie's hands. Then she took all the money Ben had as well and handed it to her. Ronnie had a fleeting thought that the Grants were rich, but didn't dwell on it too much. It was just another random thought that popped into her head along with thoughts of their dinner being cold. There were so many right now, she wasn't sure what to focus on and what not to. Margaret also took her handgun out of her purse and handed it to Ronnie as well.

"You'll need this. I know that you already have one, but most men that I've dealt with don't think of women carrying two or more weapons. Let him find this one, and you keep yours close. And, Ronnie, I want you to come back to us. I've grown quite fond of your sassy mouth."

Ronnie gave them the address and told Margaret that she didn't know if it would have much in the way of cell service, as it was really off the beaten path.

"I've not been there in ages, not since I was a child. I don't even know...I didn't know he'd take Devin. I'm so sorry, so very sorry. I don't want him hurt, Mrs. Parker. You have to know that, for as much as we fight; I would never want him harmed. I love the arrogant ass."

"Don't you worry anything about that. It'll work out, you'll see. You're going to be just fine. Of course you didn't know he'd take Devin. Insane people like him are unpredictable and stupid. He'll make a mistake and that's when it will be all over. This phone is equipped with GPS and as long as you don't take the battery out, the police will be able to track you."

"They broke down the office door at Devin's firm," Ben told them as he closed his phone. "Poor Caroline Justice is dead and there was no sign of Devin. Nickolas is headed to the basement with the police. He said to tell you that you keep your head together and you'll both be fine. He also told me to tell you that he wants you to bring his brother home. He said that he would make it up to you as soon as this is over." Ben hugged her again, telling her that this one, this hug, was from Austin and that he loved her too. They were in the managers of the restaurant's office and Ronnie couldn't remember how they had accomplished that either. She was just beginning to realize that money could make a great many things happen.

Ronnie nearly collapsed from the information about Mrs. Justice. She had liked the woman and felt responsible for her death. That poor woman had not deserved this; no one did. Tears pooled in Ronnie's eyes when she thought of her needless death.

"Now you listen here, young lady. You stay strong and come back with Devin. I don't want to lose you. You owe me some money and I plan to get it back. Now go, be safe." Margaret told her with a little shake.

Ronnie left the restaurant with just over eight hundred dollars in her pocket and was an hour into her ride now when she thought about hiding the second gun. She put it into the front of her jeans. The metal was cold, but soon warmed against her bare skin.

They were making great time, she thought. When the cabbie had balked at the address when they got closer, she showed him the cash she had and he decided to take her there despite the area and the dark streets.

The town had barely been a wide spot in the road when she was little, but still, the memories flooded her mind. The library looked closed down and the one or two trailers along the main street were not even lit very well. The houses were, for the most part, boarded up. And those that weren't had broken out windows, and grass as high as she stood was dried and swaying in the front yard. The snow that had fallen the night before had not been removed from the road and there wasn't a sign of lights anywhere the closer they got to her old home.

When the cab driver turned where she told him to, she knew she was less than five minutes from her first death. Ronnie could only hope that she could save Devin before she had her second one, for she had no doubt she was here to die.

Ronnie knew that her father had beaten her that day she had tried to kill herself. Her shooting herself in the head would not cause the sort of damage that had been done to her. Broken bodies like hers had been was something she was very familiar with and could guess what had happened. Once she was awake more, she'd listened as they explained what had happened to her.

Her jaw had been broken in three different places and had been wired shut. The doctor said he was sure that at least one of the breaks was a reinjure of something that had happened before and he had asked her how it had happened. Of course, Ronnie had said nothing. Her left arm was broken at both the wrist and the humerus. Eight ribs were broken and one of them had punctured her lung. Her pelvis had been fractured and both her legs had been broken in several places. She was told that it looked as if the robber had stomped on her several times — he must have been very angry at her for messing up his plans, the doctor had said. Ronnie was sure he had been. The gunshot wound to her head perplexed them all, but only she and her father knew the truth behind it and it had depressed her for many years that she had failed even herself.

When the driver finally stopped a mile from the house, she gave him the money she had left and asked him to please wait. As soon as he rolled up the window, he took off. Not that she could blame him. It was scary to her too. She started walking toward the house in the semi-dark, having only the moon to guide her and her horrible memories.

Devin's car was parked out front of the house and her father was leaning against it smoking a cigarette. Damned man couldn't die from cancer, could he? she thought. From what she could see of the house, it was near ruin. There was very little glass in the upper windows and the windows at the bottom, what there was of them, was dirty. With the little light shining through the house from the moon, she could see that there was grass and weeds growing through the porch boards. At one time, there had been large potted flowers in the summer and bright Christmas lights all along the windows and door for her sisters' enjoyment at Christmas. Now, the pots were a broken mess and the lights long since forgotten hung like broken fingers from the eaves in a tangled mess.

"What the fuck do you want?" He jerked around when she asked, even though she had thought he was staring right at her. "Where's Devin? I want you to let him go and I'll do whatever you want."

"So you comed, did you? That boy? Dead, or he soon will be. Can't leave any one around to interrupt us now, could I? You and I, we're gonna have us some fun. Come here." He stood up and she stood her ground.

"No. I'm not a child anymore and you don't frighten me. You've made a major mistake thinking that I would cooperate with you." She started to back up. She wasn't sure where she would go, but she would run until she couldn't anymore, with Devin on her back if need be.

"Now ain't that a shame. Oh well, we'll have to do this the hard way then. Get her!"

Before she could react, she was grabbed from behind. Foul breath and old sweat assaulted her senses. Both her arms were pinned behind her by the arm around her waist, and a gun was pointed at her head. She tried to struggle, but whoever had her was incredibly strong.

"Meet your brother, Samuel. Well, I guess he's also your nephew, beings how he's mine and Margo's brat. Wanted a girl child, but them daughters couldn't hold one in their belly long enough for it to be borned. Shame, really. Finally, the strain of it kilt your sister Holly. Margo had this one first after she got her monthlies, then nothing more lived from her body. She musta been cursed or something. Can't rightly figure out how, though. Might be her mother's doing; she always did hate me from what I doned to her. Course Samuel ain't right in the head, but he's a good grunt and he's strong as an ox. Put her out, Samuel. I gots me stuff to do."

Ronnie relaxed her stance and went limp in the man's arms. It had the effect she had hoped and he loosened his grip enough that she jerked from him, rolled on her back away from him, and freed herself. She pulled her gun and fired just as he raised his to fire at her. He dropped to the ground with a short howl.

The next bullet whizzed over her head and she would swear that she felt the heat of it going by her face. She dropped back down, rolled to her stomach, and fired at her father. He leapt out of the way and dove in the bushes, his gun going the opposite direction having been knocked from his hand by her shot. Ronnie thought that she had hit him; his body had jerked like she had.

She started to rise and realized that she had turned her ankle in a hole and it hurt. Crawling on her belly toward the trees, watching out for her father, she tried to get to safety. She never saw him come up behind her with the branch. Sudden pain flared in her head and she was out like a light.

~*Chapter 17*~

When Ronnie woke, her arms were tied above her head to a bed. She didn't know where she was at first. There was no light from anything but the windows and it was dimmer in here than it had been outside. She could make out large pieces of furniture, but not what it was. Then it hit her; she was in her sisters' old bedroom in the house where she had been born. The bed was damp and there seemed to be odors of something dead close by.

Moving her legs slightly, she could feel the small hand gun Mrs. Parker had worked into the back of her sock. He must have found the gun she used on Samuel because she could no longer feel it in her waistband. That scared her more than anything because he now had her gun. Terror ran through her at the thought of what they would do with her gun.

Devin wasn't dead. Her mind had to wrap around that thought. The only man who had treated her with...well, love, she thought. No one other than Austin and Ben had ever loved her. And when she and Devin had made love, he not only hadn't forced her, but made her feel special and cared for. She couldn't believe he was dead. It would destroy her if he was.

Crying, she looked around again, harder this time, trying to see if she was alone and, if not, would it be someone she could get to help her? If nothing else, Ronnie thought if she could piss her father off enough, he would make a mistake and she could get this over with. Now that her eyes had had time to adjust, she could make out more of the room, a room she had had to keep clean and straight more than any other room in the house.

Her sisters' room. It had been the envy of everyone who had ever been allowed to cross the threshold. Ronnie hated it and them. All the pins and ruffles had made her think someone had puked that pink belly medicine everywhere, then filled it with fluffy pillows and lace of the same color.

The dolls had to be just perfect, the beds made with all the pretty, soft pillows. Even the books that they never read had to be put in order and always back in the same direction.

Toys, all expensive, had their own place as well. And their toy boxes, each of them had their own, had been filled to overflowing with their treasures.

Their shoes and clothes needed to be put in the closet in a certain way and there had been covers for the tops of the clothes hanging there so there would be no dust on the sleeves. Ronnie never lingered in this room; it would get her beaten, especially if she touched something or looked at it too long.

Ronnie longed for the books to read, of course, something to treasure and to dream with. She had gone to the library a few times, but as no one would sign the permission slip giving her the rights to take out books, she had never taken any home. It was probably just as well. Her father would have destroyed them then punished her for it. But she did love to read.

Her own room was vastly different, which was funny since she had never had one. Ronnie mostly slept in the living room or kitchen in the winter as the room off the porch was too cold and her father didn't like paying for the doctor bills when she got sick. One year she had caught pneumonia and had nearly died. After that, she was allowed to come inside when it was below zero outside. And if he wanted to make her suffer, he would make her sleep in the twins' room so that when he and her sisters had sex, she would have to listen. He did this more and more as they got older. She hated her father for that too.

But Ronnie had liked the room on the porch. It was bright and airy and if she was very still for long periods of time at night, animals would come right out into the open and eat the grass. One time, she remembered a mother deer and her fawn had stayed for nearly twenty minutes before her family had scared them off banging around in the house, shouting for her.

Ronnie heard the scraping noise, and then a flash of light appeared to her left, bringing her back to the present with a hard thrust. The candle being lit was a soft light at first, but as the flame caught, the brilliance grew stronger and she was able to make out more of the room. Yes, she was right. This was her sisters' room. The books were gone, as were the toys, and the pretty curtains were tattered, but it was their room all right.

"Well, well, the ugly duckling has finally been found. He said he'd find you after that pitcher came out in that fancy paper. Said you were all dressed up in a purty dress that was made just for you. I ain't never had no purty dress like that for me. How'd you rate one?" Margo Frey stood over Ronnie, staring down at her.

The years had not been kind to Margo. In fact, she looked as if they had been darn right mean to her. Ronnie started to giggle at her own joke, but knew it was fear that made her think that thought. Her sister's hair was chopped off as if it had been cut by her own hand or someone else's. Her face looked haggard and used, her cheeks plump and loose. Ronnie had always thought her sisters were plump, but Margo had gotten fat, looking like she might have weighed close to three hundred pounds. Her clothes, once the pride of both girls, were now dirty and ill-fitting, holes in places and filthy too. If Ronnie had had to pick her out of a crowd, she would not have recognized her but for her blue eyes that were their father's. Everything else about her was masked in fat and poor living.

"He said you looked too much like your daddy for you to be anything but his kid. I never met him, so I just agreed like a good daughter. I've always been a good daughter, unlike you." Margo slapped Ronnie's sore ankle. "You know you might have been ugly, but there weren't no reason for you to be mean to my daddy. He provided for you and tooked care of you. No reason to be mean." Margo huffed at her.

"Margo, let me go, please? I want to go home. I don't want anything to do with him. You can have him all you want." Ronnie pulled against the ropes at her wrists and begged her sister.

"Shut up! He wants you now, not me. He'll have you too, 'cause you ain't his blood. He thinks you can give him them babies he wants and they'll turn out all right. My boy is stupid, ain't no good for nothing. He can't even get it up to satisfy me no matter what I do to try and help him. And he's got no sense. I done tried to show him how so many times, I 'bout gived up. Daddy thinks you're gonna give him his due, you hear me?" Margo paced as she ranted.

"Let me go, please? I swear I don't want him, or anything at all from him," Ronnie begged.

"I can't disobey my daddy. He says you stay, then I'm a'thinking you gotta stay. I think maybe I'ma gonna try and get me a baby from that man daddy doned bringed home. He's a looker. And he's gots himself a nice cock too."

Ronnie struggled with the ropes at her wrists. When she remembered what Margo had said, Ronnie paused in her need to get free and looked at her.

"What? What did you just say? What do you mean I'm not of his blood? I don't understand." Devin was alive and she knew he was close. Thank goodness, now all she had to...not of his blood? She must have had it wrong.

"You didn't know? Oh, that's great! He thought you runned away 'cause you found out. Said you'd found it when you was snooping around and found his pappy's gun. Well, is seems, sister dear, your daddy was the reason why Momma drank all the time. See, Daddy—my daddy wanted her to breed for him, give him girls 'cause she was so pretty and all. And you know what Daddy wants, Daddy gets. Anyway, Momma was engaged to his here guy and they was getting married soon. Daddy just stole her away the night before the big old fancy wedding." Margo sat on the narrow bed as she continued. "He had to kill your daddy, he told me, 'cause you can't leave no witnesses. But that weren't no big deal, 'cause Daddy got a two-fer. He got him a breeder and he got him you. Only thing was, you was born so ugly that he didn't want you none. He told me that he didn't like have sex with her, our momma. She wasn't tight no more like me and Holly. But he needed to keep her breeding.

"Momma only wanted her Arnold, though. Ain't that the mostest stupidest name you ever heard? Arnold Parkway. Now Daddy's got you again and once he gets a baby born outta you, he said I could kill you. Ain't that real nice of him? Only thing is, now that I sees you, I don't think he'll be wanting to stop with just one baby. He'll be wanting to fuck you all the time 'cause you look like you'd stay tight for a long time. So I done figured to kill you now."

Margo had told her this as if it were nothing at all. And to her, it probably wasn't. Ronnie's entire life had been a lie. And her mother? What kind of mother was so selfish that she would completely ignore everything and everyone around her because her heart had been broken? Ronnie decided that when she and Devin had a child, she would devote her life to making sure he or she knew that they were loved and wanted above everything else.

The knife slid out from behind Margo in slow motion. She walked up to the side of the bed and slid the knife along Ronnie's leg. She didn't just break the skin at first, but once she made the knife slide up Ronnie's thigh, then she stabbed it in deep and twisted and gouged at the wound. The cut was deep and painful and Ronnie's scream rent the cold air. Pain tore at Ronnie, making her dizzy with it.

"Yeah, while Daddy is off getting rid of that fancy car, I'm gonna chop you up into little pieces and then toss you to the hogs out back. I keeps'em hungry just in case I need to get rid of some nosy person. The mail man, the old woman at the store—she said I was too large for to be shopping in the petite section anymore." Margo twisted the knife again. "I fixed her, didn't I? Won't be telling me that I'm too fat, the stupid bitch. You can keep Holly company. Maybe tell each other how clever I am."

"He'll hurt you when he returns and finds that you've killed me. Margo, let me go and I won't say a word. I have money...and what I don't have on me, I can get for you," Ronnie told her thought her clenched teeth. "You can let me go and I'll just leave. Please, Margo, let me go, please?" She didn't know how she was going to get very far, but she had to get to Devin before it was too late.

"You know, Holly begged me too. I liked how that made me feel. Somebody beggin' me for their lives. I couldn't have her taking up anymore of Daddy's seed. I wanted to be the one to give him his little girl, not her, but when she birthed another girl child and this one seemed okay, I had to do it. That baby would have been the end of my fun with Daddy. So I kilted Holly first, then smothered that little girl child. Daddy thinks it died in birth. Holly just went in the pen, but the baby? It got a nice proper grave. Even had to go sell one of my necklaces to give her a pretty box to put her in. But it's dead, just like you're gonna be in a few more minutes."

The knife slid along Ronnie's belly, just slicing open the skin, not as deep like the one in her thigh, but no less painful. The pain nearly made her lose conciseness, but she managed to hang on; she needed to hang on. She could feel the blood leaving her leg, the wetness of it pooling under her in a warm, sticky mess.

"And now, here you are, all back and pretty to boot. I never liked you, Catalina, never. You were always too good to join Holly and me in our fun in pleasing Daddy. Why? Why didn't you want Daddy to fuck you? It feels so good. And he always gave us such pretty things afterwards." The knife left her body and Margo began playing with it in her hand. "Then when we go older, he started to show us how to please each other and we could take pleasure from him too. It was wonderful. Why didn't you want it?"

179

"Because he's a sick bastard and he made you just as sick as he is. You don't sleep with your parents, you stupid bitch. What he did to you was sick, and what's even sicker is that you don't see it," Ronnie screamed at her sister. "He's got you so brainwashed that you believe he loved you because he fucked you? You're as insane as he is. Now end me or fucking leave me to die."

The slice to her forearm was deep and Ronnie could see the bone being exposed as Margo rammed the knife into her. Blood gushed from the wound and onto her face. Dizzy now, drifting in and out quicker with the pain, Ronnie knew that she couldn't lose consciousness. She had to find Devin for his family. Taking a deep breath, fighting to stay alive, Ronnie lifted her leg high. She managed to slam her foot into Margo's chest and throw her back across the room. Ronnie had to lay there for a few precious seconds to catch her breath. That's when she noticed that the knife was near her hand.

~~~

Devin was delirious with pain. His arms were stretched high over his head and his feet barely touched the floor beneath him. There was something over his face, blocking out all light. It smelled like dirt and urine. The echoes of the room he was in amplified every little sound he heard, making him believe he was in a smallish room with very little furniture.

Devin knew that more of his ribs were broken, at least three on each side where Albert had kicked him repeatedly when they had first arrived. Devin's left arm was also broken and he thought that his wrist was badly sprained. His jaw hurt badly and he could feel that some of his teeth were loose. Even without the covering over his eyes, he was sure he wouldn't have been able to see. Between the pistol whippings he had taken in his office, and since he had been brought here, he thought he would be lucky if he didn't have permanent damage. Shifting again to take some of the weight off his leg, he cried out from the pain in his knee where Frey had hit him with a wooden ball bat after hanging him here. But that hadn't been the worst. He had also been raped.

At first, he had heard her cooing and moaning in the room. He couldn't tell where or how close she was until she touched him. She cut his shirt away. The blade of the knife had nicked him once and he felt her tongue along his skin as she licked the wound. Devin's stomach lurched again when he thought about her and her odor. When he felt the cold air hit his skin, he thought she might be finished, but then she went for his pants. This time, she took them off him, stripped him naked, and touched him everywhere as she went. He still had the gag in his mouth and when she started rubbing against his body, he nearly strangled trying to scream at her to get away. When she backed away from him, she started talking and he could hear she was talking to herself.

"Hummm, Margo, you gots to have some of that. Yes, sir, ain't no reason to let that big, fat cock go to waste. I'm gonna get him hard, then I'm gonna ride him hard. Oh yeah, that's what Margo wants. And Margo gets what Margo wants."

Devin felt his balls tighten at the thought of her touching him and he felt the bile rise again. When she grabbed his cock in her big hand and squeezed, he jerked back and twisted his already painful leg, nearly losing consciousness again. But he didn't; he couldn't. He was afraid of what she might do to him if he did. When she put her mouth over him and sucked him in, he kicked out with his better leg and knocked her over. He wasn't sure where he had hit her, but he realized she was heavy, fleshy, where his foot had connected. She grabbed his knee suddenly and twisted. Screaming in agony, the blackness swam before his eyes and he couldn't stop the tip over into it. When he came to several minutes ago, he knew that she had taken what she had wanted and he felt violated and dirty.

Drifting in and out, he thought he heard sirens again and wondered who had been hurt. He remembered Caroline then and cried for her. Muttering to himself, he hoped that she had good insurance and that her family didn't try to kill him because she worked for him. Giggling, he thought he might prefer being dead to being in pain and what his body had endured. And Veronica, his Veronica. He wished that he could have seen her again, touched her once more. He would tell her how much he loved her, wished that they had had a child, a beautiful little girl like her mommy. Devin wished he could have held her just one more time.

"Devin?" She was back, was his first thought. Well, this time, he was going to be ready for her. He had a wife, damn it, and he didn't want this woman touching him. Devin heard a scream and wondered who it was, then a gun shot. Then the blackness rose up again to claim him.

~*Chapter 18*~

Tumbling out of the bed, Ronnie grabbed her gun and pointed it at Margo who was just starting to rise. Ronnie's leg was throbbing like a toothache and her arm hung useless at her side. She had to get to Devin; she had to set him free. Margo looked at the gun and then at Ronnie.

"You can't be shooting me. I'm your sister; you can't kill your kin. It's against the Bible."

Ronnie just stared at Margo. She was insane, Ronnie decided. Insane because of the way she had been raised. Ronnie was also sure her mother drank during her pregnancy and knew that that had played some part in it as well.

"You were going to kill me, you stupid cow. And the way you've living...don't even think about quoting the Bible at me. Now, where is Devin? Tell me now and maybe I'll only shoot you in the foot and not your face. Hurry up, I don't have all night." Ronnie thought she would be lucky if she had the next ten minutes, but Margo didn't need to know that.

"Don't shoot my face, Catalina. I need to be pretty for Daddy. Here, shoot my foot; I don't need it none. Maybe I can get me one of dem fancy riding chairs to go around in. Yeah, shoot my foot. That man ain't gonna want you after this, and I done had a taste of him; he's good. We can share."

Ronnie stood up and slammed the gun across Margo's face. Rage like she had never felt surged in her blood and she had to sit back down on the bed to calm herself before she trusted herself to touch Margo again. Stripping the sheet from beneath her, Ronnie tore it into long strips and braided it together to make a tight rope. The material was rotten, so she hoped it would hold her long enough for Ronnie to find Devin and get out of here. It took her nearly ten minutes to get her sister tied to the bed.

Ronnie was coming down the stairs when she heard the sirens. They were far off, but they were coming, and she nearly shouted with joy. That was when she saw Frey go into the bathroom carrying her gun. Devin.

Ronnie moved forward as quickly as she could, the pain in her body making her see stars with every step. When she came around the corner and into the small half bath, she must have made a small sound because Frey turned just as he was putting the gun to Devin's temple and fired at her. She didn't even hesitate, but fired three times back at him. He dropped into the tub like a tumbled tree. All three bullets hit him between the eyes. She was sure he was dead before he hit the floor.

Before she could go to Devin, the police rushed the room. She was knocked to the ground on her belly and someone was yanking her arms behind her. She cried out; the pain rippled along her body like a fast moving freight train.

"Don't move. We need to secure the place. Anyone else in the house besides you three?" the man whispered in her ear.

"Upstairs. A woman tied to the bed. She's meaner than a snake, so be careful. And I killed a man outside. Samuel Frey, my stepbrother/nephew, hell, he could be my cousin for all I know." She giggled manically and closed her mouth tight. It probably wouldn't do for her to lose it right now. "Can you please let go of me? I hurt and I want to see Devin."

"There's a doctor outside who says he's his brother. Would it be all right if he comes in and has a look at him first?"

Ronnie wanted to cry and to laugh. Damon would make sure Devin lived. She couldn't talk over the knot in her throat and simply nodded. She heard the officer talk to someone and then he gently rolled off her. Ronnie stayed where she was; she hurt too much to move right then.

Damon went past her without a glance and straight into the bathroom where Devin was hanging. She couldn't make out the words, but it was enough to know that Devin was speaking, screaming really, something about Frey and a woman touching him. Ronnie rolled to her back and clawed her way to standing.

Devin was babbling and his brother was talking softly to him. Ronnie stepped forward and noticed that, at some point, Nickolas had come in too. They were both lowering Devin to the floor as gently as they could, but he was still screaming at the pain. Ronnie leaned forward and touched his forehead.

"Oh, Devin. I'm so sorry."

His scream tore through her. "Get her away from me! Please, Damon, don't let her touch me again. Nicky, throw her out; I don't want her to touch me. She raped me; please get her away from me."

She backed up so quickly she hit the wall behind her and froze. Neither man made a move to stop her when she turned and limped from the room, Devin's accusations still loud in the air.

He didn't want her. Just as Margo had said, Devin no longer wanted her after he truly found out what she had come from.

Ronnie stumbled out the door and onto the porch. Leaning over the rail, she threw up. No one noticed her, or they didn't care, so when she had sicked up everything, she simply staggered away into the night, numb with grief, her body's pain only secondary to her broken heart.

The sun was just coming up when Ronnie stopped moving. It wasn't so much that she had stopped, but she just ran out of energy. Ronnie slid down the tree and looked around. If anyone had asked her what she had been doing since leaving the house, she wouldn't have been able to tell them. She wouldn't have been able to tell them one thing she had seen, one thing she had heard, and nothing that she had thought of either. Closing her eyes, she fell into a dreamless sleep and slipped once again into the nightmare, another one that she would have to relive night after night. This one was Devin telling her to get away from him.

The next time she woke, the sun was fully up. At some point, she must have rolled over because now she was lying on her back, the sun full in her face. She thought if she lay there long enough, she would be covered in the snow that was just coming down and they wouldn't find her until spring. Then she thought of Austin and Ben.

Fanning her hands over her shirt and pants, ignoring the harsh pain, she found her cell phone and opened it. A few seconds later, she closed it again. What did she say to them and what would they say to her? Crying softly, she knew that she had to call them if for no other reason than to find out if Devin had lived. Opening the phone again, she continued to cry as she pressed the numbers to call him. When Austin answered, she immediately told him not to say anything.

"All right. We are still waiting for word about Ronnie. We don't know if she's all right or not. Have you heard anything?" Ronnie burst into tears.

"I'm hurt, I think badly, but I...I'm numb. Is Devin all right? I know that he hates me, but I need to know."

"He's in surgery. The doctors give him a very good chance of full recovery. His injuries are bad, but not life threatening. That's where I am now, at the hospital—Ohio State. Can you come here?"

"No, I can't move, don't even know if I want to really." Ronnie heard his sharp intake of breath and felt bad. "I don't know where I am. Somewhere in Nashport, I think. My arm...I've lost a lot of blood and I'm dizzy. Are you sure he's all right?"

"Yes, I'm sure. Let me send someone to come and get you if you won't come here. I can take care of things for you. You know that I will."

"Austin, I killed two men tonight. I killed them in cold blood and I won't do that to you and Ben. And Devin said...he told them . . ."

"I'm well aware of all that. And I can assure you that I don't give a shit. Let me send someone to get you. Please?" The last word was a whisper and her heart clenched at it.

She didn't think she could move, but she knew that if she didn't let him, Austin would call out the National Guard to find her. She tried to sit up, but it was just too much effort. She hurt more now that she knew Devin was going to be all right.

"Do you know where Nashport is? It's a small town between Dresden and Zanesville. There's a little post office off the main road; I can see it right now. It'll be about five miles from my old house. Can you find it?"

187

"You know that I will. I'm calling a friend now and you'll go with him. His name is Sheppard, Thomas Sheppard. He'll know what to do when he gets to you. I'll see you later, all right?"

"Yes. Austin, I'm so sorry. I'll make this up to you and Ben, I promise."

"When I see you later we'll talk. Take care and I'll talk to you later. Good night." He disconnected the call, but not before she could hear the small sob in his voice.

Ronnie didn't close the phone, but turned it over and worked at the back panel to get the battery out. Her fingers were sore from the cuts from the knife and her blood made things slippery, but she finally got it off and took the battery out. She wasn't sure anyone would care where she was other than Austin and Ben, but she didn't want to see anyone right now. Closing her eyes again, thinking the snow was getting heavier, she drifted off again.

~~~

Devin woke three days later. He was in horrendous pain and had to fight hard to stay awake long enough to see that his mother and brothers were in the room with him. His mother kissed his cheek and he slipped away again. His last thought was where Veronica was, but he didn't get a chance to ask.

The next time he woke, he could hear his brother Byron arguing and shouting and he turned his head to tell him to shut up when the pain hit him. He took a deep breath and that was when his brother Spencer noticed that he was awake. Byron told whoever he was talking to that he needed to go and hung up.

"Veronica," Devin finally managed to ask.

"The doctor said you could have some water if you want it. But you have to take it slow and easy." The straw was in his mouth in the next instant. The cold water felt like ambrosia. Byron took it away much too quickly.

"Veronica? Where is she?" He was glad that he had taken a drink, but now his belly felt like it was going to toss it back up. He had to take several deep breaths before he thought he could breathe normal again. He looked up at Byron and saw him glance at something, or someone, on the other side of them. Devin would have turned to look too, but it was too painful.

"She's gone. They've been trying to find her since the shooting. The police said she was in the house when they went in to get you both and after making sure the house was secured, she disappeared." His mother. She was who Byron had looked at.

"Hurt? Is she hurt?" He licked his lips and had to try again. "Was she hurt that they saw?"

"There was evidence that shows that she may have been stabbed several times. There was blood in the room where her sister was and more on the stairs and porch. The snow coming so soon after they discovered she was missing has hampered their efforts to find her. Dogs couldn't find her in the deep snow." Devin looked at his brother and noticed that he wouldn't look him in the face. Something else had happened.

"Tell me. Tell me what you're not. Please, Byron, I need her."

"I've talked to Austin and Ben. I think they know where she is, but they won't say. A signed confession came to the police station yesterday telling them what had happened and how she had killed the two men the police found and what she did to her sister. There is also an accounting of what her sister Margo said to her about her father and the other sister, Holly. She...Veronica isn't her first name. Her last...it's not

189

even Frey, not really. Her first name is Catalina and according to the DNA records, she isn't Frey's daughter either, but a man named Albert Parkway's. The Parkways had filed a missing person's report twenty-nine years ago. He's Ronnie's real father."

"Why won't they tell you where she is, Byron? What else aren't you telling me? You have to tell me."

Byron looked over at his mother again and nodded. He leaned down and kissed Devin's forehead and left the room. His mother walked around to the other side of the bed where Byron had been standing. She laid something on the bed and looked at it instead of him.

"You told the police she raped you. Devin, you wouldn't let her near you when they found you. You were out of your mind with pain, Damon said. Nicky said that he wanted to talk to her, but you needed medical treatment right away and when he went to find her, she had already disappeared. She sent this to me with a check two days ago, along with a copy of the report she sent to the police. The note is from Ben. In it he said he nearly had it cleaned for you, but thought you should see what she gave up to get you out of that house." Margaret reached down and picked up the jewelry box and opened it for him.

The ring was there nestled inside. And it was covered in blood. Ronnie's blood, he was sure. Devin looked up at his mother who was crying openly now.

"They used this blood to compare her DNA; there was so much of it then. She killed that man because I told her to. I told her to kill him and to make sure you were safe. Nicky told her the same thing and now look. Austin won't tell me where she is or if she's hurting or needs me. Every time I look at this ring, I think about her face when you slipped it...Oh Devin, that poor girl. What have I done to her?"

Things were coming back to him in snatches now. He remembered Margo coming to him and touching him. Devin remembered her voice; Veronica's, when she came into the room where he was being held. He didn't remember much after that or just before, but he must have said those things. He could remember being frightened and in so much pain. His brothers pulling him up then lying him down on the cold floor, the way his arms hurt first from being over his head so long, then the pain of them being hurt. He looked down at himself then and had to close his eyes at what he saw.

Both arms were in casts. His left leg was in some sort of pulley system that held it up, immobile. His right ankle was resting on a pillow also in a cast and he could feel his ribs pull every time he took even a shallow breath. His vision was slightly blurry and his jaw hurt, but not like it had. He wondered what other injuries he had and then decided that he might be better off not knowing — at least for right now.

"I need to find her. I need to talk to her. Can you call Austin for me? Tell him I want to talk to her, that I need to talk to her? Beg him for me, please, Mom. I love her so much and I can't be without her. Tell him I love her for me."

"It's late, love. I'll call him first thing in the morning, I swear. And if he won't talk to you, then I'll have to resort to other means. I don't know what I'll do, but if you want to talk to her, then you will. Rest now. We'll work this out in the morning."

Devin was wide awake and waiting for his mother when she came back in at seven o'clock in the morning. He had refused pain medication so that he would not drift off and be put off, and now he was hurting in every part of his body. He needed Veronica and he needed her now.

Listening to his mom, he didn't think she was having much luck with Austin either. She was in near tears when she hung up the phone. When she had to go to the bathroom before speaking, he wanted to howl out his frustrations. When she came out, her eyes were red and swollen and her nose looked like it was slightly runny.

"They won't tell me. Austin said that she promised them if any of us showed up, they were never see her again either. They don't want to risk that for anyone, especially you. They said to tell you to let it go, that she is going to be okay and that she feels no ill will toward you or the rest of the family. Devin, I'm so sorry. I've tried everything."

"I know, Mom, but I'm not giving up. There has to be someone who knows where she is. And I damned well am going to find her."

Devin had to find her. He was in love with her and he was sure that love like he had for her would never come around again. Devin pulled on the cord to call the nurse shortly after his mother left. He was in too much pain to think, but as soon as he could, he would think of something to get her back.

~*Chapter 19*~

Byron knew he was taking a big chance, but he needed to see for himself that she was all right—and if he could talk her into coming back with him, then that would be all the better for all of them. He hated that his mother was crying over this and that Devin was hurting so bad that he was nearly inconsolable.

The nursing home was in the middle of Virginia. He had been driving most of the night and he was exhausted. Austin told him that if he screwed this up for him that he would have a contract put out on his life so fast he would never know what hit him. Byron believed him too. There was something about the glint in the older man's eye that had scared him not just a little. He pushed open the door to her room and was temporarily shocked at what he saw.

She was pale, but what got him the most was how much weight she had lost in such a short time. Her face was bandaged up near her jaw and there was a cast of sorts on her right arm. He couldn't see the rest of her body, but he could make out the cast on her leg as well. An IV pole held up several bags of liquid, two clear and one yellow. He could also smell the acidy smell of vomit along with the septic smell of disinfectant. Her eyes were closed, but he could tell that she was not sleeping.

"Ben called me ten minutes ago and told me you were coming. I promised him that I would listen, but I never promised him that I would speak to you. Tell me what you have to say then get out. I have an appointment at four o'clock and I don't like to miss it."

Byron walked into the room and let go of the breath he didn't realize he was holding. He laid the box of chocolates on the table that Austin had given him to bring her and sat in the chair closest to the bed. He reached up to take her hand and after a second of letting him hold it, she pulled away and opened her eyes. They stared at one another for a long time, not saying anything.

"You look like hell. I guess you look better than the other guy since he's dead, but you would run a close second. How are you, Ronnie, really?"

"You Grant men have such a way with women, it's small wonder you all aren't married. Tell me whatever it is and leave me alone, Byron. I don't know what you told Austin, but he must have thought it was something to tell you where I am."

"Devin doesn't know I'm here. No one does but Austin and Ben. I told them—no, I promised them that I would keep your secret even if you wouldn't come home with me. Devin is in pain. His wounds are healing, but his heart it broken. My mom cries daily wondering if you need her. Nicky feels guilty for telling you to bring Devin back with no more help than that. I miss you. I like you very much and love the way you put Devin in a twist."

"He told those men that I...it doesn't matter. He'll soon forget about me, I'm sure. He's rich and good-looking; there will be women flocking around him in no time. If you're finished, I'd really like for you to...open the curtain for me. Quickly, before it's too late."

Byron didn't hesitate, but jumped to the window and pulled open the curtain for her. He could hear them now, and seeing them put a smile on his face. Looking back at Ronnie, he saw her straining to see them too. He walked over to the bed and picked her up in his arms slightly so that she wouldn't have to stretch so much.

Three little kids, a girl and two boys were playing in the snow. They all looked to be under the age of six or seven. There was a blond cocker spaniel running around them leaping and yapping at them while they played.

"They come out every day at four. The first time I saw them was my first day here when I had opened my eyes. Do you have kids?" she asked him softly.

"No, but I have a niece, Meggie, and then there are Nicky's boys, and my stepfather had two boys that we all consider our nephews." She squirmed slightly and he adjusted her and put her back on the bed more comfortably.

"I held one of Mr. Grant's boys. I don't know which one. It was the first time I'd ever even touched a kid before. Morgan got huffy with me when I called him an 'it.' He didn't cry or anything. I think it would be better to have a dog, like that one. I've never had one of those either, a pet, I mean, but I bet it would be considerably more loyal. You can put me down now; they'll be going in soon." He settled her back in the bed and repositioned her pillow under her arm.

Up close like this, he could see the bruises on her face, faint but still swollen. There was also a tinge of blood on her arm where the bandage was. He was concerned, but said nothing. He could tell she was still hurting. Both of them were, and he wanted, no, he needed to set things right.

"Ronnie, would you please come back with me to Ohio? I'm not asking for Devin, not even my mother, though I'll deny that I said that if anyone asked. I want you to come back for Austin. When I saw him yesterday, he looked aged. Ben said he was worried about him. They love you very much. Hell, I love you too. I know they'd do anything for you, baby. But they told me that you should talk to Devin too. Talk to Devin for me, please?"

"I don't know. I love...I loved him so much, Byron, and he told them to keep me away from him. I never touched him that way. We had sex, but it was never...I never took anything from him." Tears streamed down her face and she turned away from him.

Byron hurt for her—for them both, her and Devin. She had endured so much and had done so much for his family that he wanted to take her into his arms and hold her. He wanted to put her in a safe place and keep her protected for all time.

"She raped him, you know? Your sister, the one...Margo, she raped him. While he was tied to that beam in the bathroom, she came in and performed fellatio on him. He doesn't remember talking to you at the end. He was in a great deal of pain, Damon said, and when he heard your voice, it must have scared him a little. Devin is seeing a psychiatrist for it. He has nightmares nearly every night."

He could see her pale even more and nearly felt bad for the extra pain he caused her, but he knew that if she came back with him, she would never regret it. He would make sure of it. And he was certain that Devin loved this woman. And as he loved Devin, he would do nearly anything to make him happy too.

"Margo said that he wasn't my father, that Albert Frey kidnapped my mother when she was pregnant with me. His sole purpose was to have her 'breed' little girls for him. What kind of person does that to a family?"

"He wasn't. Your father, I mean. DNA proved it. Your mother is dead; I don't know if Austin told you or not. There are other things, as well, things I think you should know. The FBI has been called in and they are using dogs to search the grounds around the house where you grew up. When they brought the dogs...when you came up missing, they used something in the house to have them search for you. They couldn't, of course, because the stench of death was too much for them. There were bodies, Ronnie. So far, they've uncovered about twenty-six, all children. There were also a few young women. Identification has been difficult, but they are working through them. They are looking for your other sister, Holly Frey. They've tried to ask Margo, but she has gone over the deep end—they have her locked up and on suicide watch."

Byron watched her shift again, trying to hide the tears. This time, he sat on the bed with her and held her hand. She didn't pull away. They both looked out the window, either seeing anything beyond their thoughts.

"Holly is dead. Margo killed her then fed her to the pigs she said she kept hungry for that purpose. There might be a mailman and a shop clerk there as well. I don't know how you would go about confirming that. There was a baby, an infant, I'm assuming. She was buried in a casket, though I don't know if that's true or not. Holly had given birth to her and Margo didn't want her to give our fa...her father a girl when she couldn't."

The nurse came in and set a tray on the table behind him. Byron could smell the food on it and even though he wasn't hungry, he thought even the smell alone would turn his stomach. He turned when the nurse lifted the lids. "Gross" was all he could think of. He looked back at Ronnie and she hadn't moved.

"Mrs. Pride, you need to eat all of this today. The doctor said that if you didn't start eating soon, he would put a tube down your throat again. Not only is that not comfortable, but it's also going to keep you in here for a few more days. Try to eat some of this please?"

"Will it be all right if I go and get her something and bring it back? She kind of likes weird foods and I'd love to bring it in for her." Byron turned on the charm and had the nurse eating out of his hand. She took the offensive tray out of the room and giggled at him so much that he had to chuckle.

"I do not eat weird foods. What a thing to tell someone. She probably thinks I eat worms or something. And now I have no food."

"Well, Mrs. Pride—so not going there, what can I go and get you? And that stuff smelled like shit. If you want, I can go get her and tell her to bring it back." He grinned when she shuddered.

When Byron returned an hour later, Ronnie was on the phone. He pulled out the two subs he had gotten and opened her pop. She turned up her nose at him, but took it anyway. He knew that she drank tea, but he wasn't sure what kind to get her. When she was finished with her call, she picked up her sandwich.

"That was Austin. I'm going to come home, but I don't get out of here for another two days. I'm not sure if I want to see Devin right now. I'm not sure I want to see anyone right now. You...thank you, Byron. And you can take this back with you." She pushed the box of candy back at him.

"What, you don't like chocolate? I thought it was a food group for most women. Don't tell me, you'd rather have a basket of fruit?"

"No, I love chocolate. Austin sent this because of you. Go ahead, open it. I'm supposed to tell you something when you do."

He was almost afraid to. Byron tentatively pulled the box toward him and pulled off the lid. The white padded paper on the top was written on, but before he could read it, Ronnie snatched it away. His breath whooshed out. Slowly, he raised his eyes to Ronnie.

"Austin says, 'Fuck this up and she is to use this on your sorry ass, love Austin.' He said that I was to show you how much he trusted you with where I was."

Instead of dark chocolate and nuggets like the box suggested there might be inside, there was a gun. And not just any gun either, but a Glock with two extra clips that looked to be full. He carefully put the lid back on the box and gently pushed it to her. He decided right there that he would never underestimate her again. Ronnie was a very scary woman.

Byron leaned over the table and brushed his mouth over hers. He was going to love having her back; he was looking forward to having her as his sister-in-law too. Now, he just had to figure out what to tell his brother.

~~~

Devin was nearly asleep the next night when Byron walked in. He knew the moment that he saw him that something had happened. Almost afraid of the answer, he asked.

"I saw Ronnie yesterday. I'm not going to tell you where or how I found her. Suffice it to say she is one scary broad when she wants to be. But she'll be coming home in a few days."

"Will she come and see me?" Devin watched as his brother paced the room.

"Honestly, I don't know. You hurt her, and even though I explained what happened, she's still hurt. Devin, if you hurt her like this again, there will be no stopping me from kicking your ass all the way to hell and back, not even Mom. Ronnie looks...she looks wounded, and I don't mean the wounds on her body—though those are bad enough—but she looks like someone ripped her heart out and stomped it."

He didn't know what to say. Thank you seemed so inadequate, but he said it anyway.

"There's something I'm going to do for her and you'll just have to live with it, literally. I'm buying her a dog, a puppy. She told me she's never had a pet and I'm going to get one for her. You have a problem with that?"

"No. Ummm, can I at least help you pick it out?" Devin wanted to laugh, but he thought his brother might just follow through on the ass kicking threat and he was in enough pain as it was.

"Nope. I'm going to get her a cocker spaniel—a pretty little blond one and I'm going to have a bow put in her hair for her. Oh, and she wants kids. Ronnie wants kids. Maybe I'll let you get those for her." With that, Byron left the room.

Devin lay back on his bed and smiled. She was coming home and she wanted children. Then he frowned. He hoped Byron was kidding about the dog; he didn't care for dogs in general.

~*Chapter 20*~

She was exhausted. The ride from Virginia to Ohio had taken a lot out of her and she wasn't even home yet. Ronnie wished now that she had taken Austin up on him wanting to pay for her ticket on a plane rather than taking a bus. The taxi was still an hour from home and she was fighting back the tears as hard as she could. It was a week after the New Year and she was home.

The driver pulled up in front of her home and she couldn't move. There was no way she was going to be able to climb out of the vehicle and then up the stairs. She sat there in the back seat and sobbed while he ran to the house to get someone. Austin came running out in his shirt sleeves. It was the first time she had seen him since she had been hurt. Byron was right; he had aged.

"I'm so sorry. I can't...if you let me sit here, I'll take a pain pill and when it kicks in, I'll come inside. I didn't realize it would be so hard."

"Nonsense. Byron, pick the girl up and bring her inside. Her room is all ready for her. Come on now, I've got the driver and your things. Ben has been cooking all day and he has all your favorites ready. That's it; her room is just that way."

She was in the house and in her bed before she could realize that Byron was there. She took the two pain pills and within ten minutes, was drifting off again. Ronnie vaguely remembered something, but it was gone before the thought completed.

The room was semi-dark when she woke. Her body hurt, especially her leg, but she thought she could get up. She was sitting up to do so when she heard someone clearing their throat.

"Austin said to tell you if you step one foot out of that bed he'll beat your ass so hard you'll think twice about it again. I'm not really sure what that means, but I don't think I'd mess with him today. He seems to be a tad stressed."

Devin. She reached over to turn on the bed side lamp and was ready to blast him one when she turned back to look at him. Her heart clenched in her chest.

"I'm so sorry, Devin. I never thought he'd hurt someone else. He hurt you bad, didn't he?" His face was bruised, but not nearly as bad as she was sure it had looked. There were stitches over his eye and his lip, but it was him sitting in the wheel chair that hurt her the most. Both his legs were in casts, as well as his arm. She wondered how he was even here.

"He hurt us both, love, but he's gone now. Thanks to you. I never thanked you for—shit—for saving my life. If you had not shot him—damn it—if you had not shot him...oh bugger it all. Here. Byron and I got this for you. She's killing me; every time she moves she gets me right in the balls." The furry little ball landed on the bed with a small bounce.

Before Ronnie could ask, the small fur ball was all over her. A puppy! Suddenly, she was being licked and nipped at and the poor little thing was going to wiggle herself in half she was so excited. Ronnie burst into tears when she cuddled her close to her neck and the little thing settled down.

"You got me a puppy? She's beautiful. What's her name? I've never had a dog before. Oh, Devin, thank you so much." She wanted to get up to go over to him, but just as she started to rise again, her door opened.

"You move one toe off that bed and I swear to you, I will never let you out of my sight again. Let me help you. Where are you headed?" Austin boomed as he came into the room with Ben close behind.

"Bathroom. Look, Austin, a puppy. Can I keep her? Ben, don't you just love her? Oh look at her; she's all worn out from her excitement." Austin grunted and glared at Devin. Ben set the tray down, picked up the dog and snuggled him.

"What's her name? She needs something regal, I think. Did she come with papers, Devin?" Ben smiled at them both and as soon as Austin picked up Ronnie, he started straightening the bed.

"Yes, she had a pedigree. Nothing but the best, Byron said. Her name on the papers is Danielle's Dream. I think the owner was calling her Dani. I would guess that you could call her what you want," Devin said while he petted the little pup that was now asleep on his lap.

"Dani it is. I'll be right back. If you need to leave, I'll understand." She actually was torn between wanting him to leave and wanting him to stay. Ronnie closed the door with a soft snap and did her business.

When she opened the door, both Austin and Ben were gone. She moved further into the room and noticed that Devin was in her bed. She didn't know what to do.

"Come on, love. I'm in no shape to make love to you, as much as I need you right now. But I do want to hold you.

And talk to you. I've got so much to explain, so much I want to tell you. Please?"

She hobbled to the bed using one crutch and settled down on the very edge. She had to work at getting her leg up and into the bed, but with Devin's help, she was lying stiffly next to him. He rolled her to her side and pulled her over him as best he could with his arm in a cast and his wrist bound on the other arm. She had never felt anything so wonderful in her life. She just breathed him in.

"I'm sorry about what I said to you at the house. I was out of my mind in pain. That woman, she...she did things to me. Things that I still can't...I have nightmares still. I couldn't see, the blindfold and the swelling...but I knew it wasn't you. I know your touch, your scent. I love you, Veronica. I've never...please don't toss me out. Let me stay here with you tonight. I need to hold you, know for real that you're safe and with me."

"All right, Devin, you can stay. I know we have to talk, but you're right. Let's just hold each other for now."

"I want to get the grim part over with first, if that's all right. Byron said that he told you about the bodies at the house. There are over thirty now. They're tracking down the families of some of the victims. DNA has helped, but not in all cases. The missing mailman, Dale Curtis, could be one of victims. There were three clerks that came up missing a few years ago and the police are wondering if maybe they all met the same fate as Margo described to you. They've kept all that out of the paper for now. I've talked to the authorities and they have asked to speak to you. I'm representing you for the present and they are going ask you what you knew about your step father's activities. I explained that there might not be too much you could help them with because you had been fairly young when you left home. They are also looking into the 'break-in' that happened to you when you were hurt."

"I remember Mr. Curtis. He was a nice young man and he always brought me a piece of candy and gave it to me when no one was looking. Poor man." Ronnie shifted over onto her back, but Devin pulled her back again. "My father...Mr. Frey beat me that morning. He came back for some reason and I'm not sure what happened, but he beat me. I couldn't go back there, not again. When the doctors started talking about my progress and that I'd be going home in a few weeks, I knew that I had to make arrangements to get away. It was my only chance." She ran her fingers over his chest and watched his even breathing.

"I think in light of things that we've discovered, you were right for leaving when you did. He probably would have killed you if you had gone back home. How did you escape?"

"You're right, he was planning it. He told me once when he visited me in the hospital that he was tired of me costing him money on hospital bills, that if I didn't want to be his daughter fully then it was time I was 'made gone.' So I left. I hid in one of the lunch warmers that sat in the hall when they brought us our meals. I didn't think it would be so hot in it, and nearly got out, but then it began to move. As soon as it stopped, I slipped out and left. I spent the first month sleeping wherever I could. It was warm and a lot of people had loungers in their yards with towels. It was all right unless it rained. I started stealing where I could, hording it and making myself a stash. I knew that the towels and chairs weren't going to last forever so I'd take stuff. I hated it, but I was determined I was not going back even if it killed me."

"How long were you on the streets before Austin found you? He said he thought it wasn't very long."

"A little over a year. I don't have any idea how I survived that first winter. My father would make me sleep on the porch year round when I lived at home, only coming in when it got below zero out. So that helped me some, I guess. And there were people that helped, strangers mostly. I had to do things I'm not proud of. I ate from dumpsters, I shoplifted. But I made it. A lot of the kids I was on the street with didn't. When Austin found me, I had been tossed out of an abandoned house because they were tearing it down."

Ronnie wiped away the tears that were falling. She hated to cry and hated more that she seemed to be doing it more and more lately. When his arm tightened around her, she buried her face in his neck.

"I love you. I don't care what you had to do to survive, baby. I only care about the woman that you've become. You are a vibrant, intelligent woman who is a force to be reckoned with. I want to spend the rest of my life with you, have children with you, raise that ridiculous dog with you. I want to wake up next to you every morning and sleep with you every night."

"Oh, Devin. I love you too. These past weeks have been so hard not knowing where you were, if you were okay, if you hated me."

"I could never hate you. I could be mad at you, pissed off, but I could never hate you. Marry me, let's get rid of that horrible man once and for all and change your name to Grant. We'll be Grant and Grant—you can even be the top billing." He grinned when he looked down at her and she kissed him.

Moaning, he deepened the kiss and started to roll over onto her and had to stop. His casts were heavy and cumbersome and he couldn't touch her. Ronnie started laughing and was soon laughing so hard she had tears streaming down her face. He looked so fierce that it was funny.

"You just wait until I'm better. Once I am, I'm going to make love to you for a solid three days before I let you leave the bedroom. Will you marry me, Veronica? Please?"

~*Chapter 21*~

May fifteenth dawned bright and beautiful. Devin thought he was going to be sick. Every time he looked out into the church, it looked as if two hundred more people had shown up. He was an attorney for Christ's sake. He could talk to anyone, talk to them for hours if need be. So why was this bothering him so much? He rubbed his belly again and looked over at Nicky who was smiling that stupid smile again.

Every time he looked at his brother, he was on his phone. He wondered again what sort of game he could be playing that would demand so much of his attention. Then realized that Nicky was probably checking stock quotes or something. Byron was doing the same thing. He was going to kill them both before this was over.

"Hey, I have something for you. I was going to keep it, but I thought you'd like to have it. Hang on while I get it out of the other room." Byron took off toward the door.

"If it's another fucking dog, I'm going to murder you. Dani takes up more room on the bed than I do and every time I kiss Veronica, she growls at me." Devin wouldn't tell anyone, but he actually loved the little thing. And if he could see Veronica's face light up like it did every time the dog licked her, then he would have hundreds of them in his home—no, their home.

"You shouldn't say the 'f' word in a church, Uncle Devin. Grandma is going to be mad at you. Again," Jacob, Dan's grandson, told him in a stage whisper.

"She won't know if you don't tell her. Besides, it's my wedding day. I think I'm exempt today. Don't you think?" Devin ruffled the kid's hair.

"No, I think she'll be mad and I won't have to tell her. She knows everything." Devin couldn't argue with him there. His mom did have an uncanny way of finding things out.

His phone ringing startled him. Devin smiled when he saw who was texting him. Maybe she was going to say they should just elope.

"You're brothers said you are getting cold feet. True?"

"No. Nervous, but want you to be my wife."

"Me too. Your wife, I mean. How do you feel about being a dad too?"

"I'd love it. Want to start on that tonight? It's been a long time."

"Last night is not a long time. And you already have a head start. Found out today."

Devin stared at the line on his phone for a whole minute. He wasn't sure how much longer he would have continued, but her next line prompted him to answer her.

"Devin?? Are you mad?"

"God, no!! I love you. Really? We're going to be parents?"

"Yes. Around Christmas time. Damon said he would be my doctor. Okay?"

"Oh, V, I love you. I love you. I love you. I love you."

"Tee -hee, I love you too. Let's get married."

Byron came toward him just as he was closing the phone. He couldn't help it; he grabbed his brother and kissed him soundly on the mouth. He was going to be a daddy, and without Byron's help, it would never have happened.

"Save it for the honeymoon, you dork. Here, I got this from Austin at the charity thing before Christmas and I thought you'd like it. I don't think you would have appreciated it so much back then as you do now." Byron tore off the paper and showed him.

Devin had to lean against the wall or fall over. It was Veronica as a child. He looked up at his brother and asked him when it had been painted.

"Austin said that her father, Frey, showed up one day asking for Catalina. She must have heard him and ran away. They found her in the garden waiting for him. Told them that if he was going to kill her, she wanted it to smell pretty when he did."

"She had heather planted on her father's grave from headstone to foot. I didn't understand until now. She told me that there was too much evil coming from his grave that she wanted it to smell pretty." Devin picked up the framed picture after handing Byron his cell phone. "Read Veronica's last texts."

He knew when his brother got to the baby part because he whooped so loud one of the ushers opened the door to check on them. Devin didn't even look up, but continued to stare at the portrait. He was going to hang it in his office as soon as they got back from their honeymoon. The door opened again, this time the minister telling them it was time.

Meggie came out first; she looked so beautiful in her long pink dress. Her dark hair was pulled back in a fat braid and she had pretty little daisies braided in it. She was tossing flowers on the carpet and looking for all the world like a little princess.

Next came Sophie, a girl that Ronnie was going to college with. She was a very pretty girl and, of course, Byron had already asked her out several times only to be turned down every time. Devin thought he could like the girl except she had this laugh that grated on his very last nerve. But she looked pretty in her long gown of blue.

The bodice was darkest and as the dress fell to the floor, the color faded to a very light blue. The dress was sleeveless and she wore long, elbow-length gloves. Her hair had been pulled back in a coronet and daisies like the ones that Meggie was tossing out of her basket were braided in her hair too. The bouquet was of calla lilies and honeysuckle with long ribbons of white and blue.

When the wedding march sounded, Devin took a deep breath. They had all been very quiet about the dress Veronica was going to wear and he was excited to see her dressed in it. Spencer had been the only one to have seen it; not even his mom had been able to get a peek. When Veronica came around the corner on Austin's and Ben's arms, everyone else could have been stripped naked and having an orgy on the floor for all he saw of them. She was beautiful. More beautiful than she had ever been to him.

She didn't have on a veil for, which he was grateful for; he could see the happiness on her face and the smile that lit up the room. And he would swear she was sparkling. She wore a tiara in her hair, which was hanging down and curly. He had asked if she could wear it down for him and he was so glad that she had. The dress was white silk and glittered off the candles and lights throughout the room. It molded to her body, fitting over her slim curves and full breasts like it had been painted on her. The bodice was bare to the top of her breasts and the way they spilled over the top made his mouth water and his cock twitch in his tux. With each step she took, he could see the full length of her leg from the split up the side that was cut to just about mid-thigh were he could see the top of her tight, high stockings and the navy blue garter there.

His brother Byron poked him in the back when he didn't move to take her from her parents. The little laughter in the room made him realize that he had been staring just a little too long. When she was finally in his arms, he cupped the back of her head and kissed her, hard and fast. The minister cleared his throat and winked at him.

"Pay attention, young man. You have the rest of your lives together. Now, if you are quite finished, what say you we get you two married?"

Devin nodded, but didn't take his eyes from Veronica's. He didn't know if he would ever be "finished" with her.

"Dearly beloved, we are…"

And just like that, they were married.

~~~

Ronnie looked around the room in awe. She was married—and not just married, but also pregnant. Rubbing her hand over the flat surface of her belly, she smiled brighter. A baby, Devin's baby.

"So, when were you going to tell me I was going to be a grandfather? Don't look at me like that, Ronnie Grant. I'm old, not dead. You've been ill for over two weeks." Austin was dancing the father-daughter dance with her and she smiled up at him.

"I was going to tell you later, I swear. I just found out the morning. I thought I had the flu and didn't want to be sick in Paris. A baby, Austin. I'm having a baby." She flushed when someone turned and looked at her.

"Yes, that happens when you go at it like bunnies all the time. I suppose this was planned? I'd hate to have to kill your husband now that he's made an honest woman of you." She looked up at him and he kissed her on the cheek. "I'm very happy for you, sweetheart. I'm not happy about watching that damned dog for two weeks while you're gone. He couldn't have bought it for you after you were married and home now, could he? Oh well, I'll just have to figure out a way to make him sorry. Maybe I'll make him do all my legal work for me for free. That would be worth it."

Ronnie laughed and rested her head on his shoulder. She loved this man so much, he and Ben both. And when Ben came up behind her and slipped his arms around her waist, she turned and held them both. She had something to ask them first before she traded partners and danced with Ben.

"This baby will never know the things I had to live with growing up and it will never be unloved, I know that. But I was wondering if he or she could call you both grandda? I know it's a lot to—"

She was suddenly being swung around the room. Next, Ben plucked her up and hugged her tightly against him, smiling brightly. She smiled; she guessed they were okay with it.

Her next dance was with Devin. They held each other so close she could feel his breath on her neck every time he inhaled. It was driving her crazy with need. When he pressed his erection into her again, she looked up at him and flushed. Need rippled in his eyes and she was suddenly wet with her own need. He leaned down and nipped at her ear; a shudder ran over her body.

"If I can't find a place to take you very soon, I'm not going to be responsible for the show these people get when I toss up this lovely dress and fuck you right here. My cock has been hard since you came out of the back room and started walking toward me. I want to suckle on your nipples while I pound my cock deep into your pussy."

"Devin, please." She didn't know if she could say anymore. All she could think about was his hot words being whispered in her ear as his cock brushed over her mound.

"There's a little room just off the front of this place. I saw it when we were having our rehearsal dinner. Go there and take off your panties. I'm going to take you hard and fast before anyone misses us, all right?" He kissed her hard before she could answer and then stepped away.

Ronnie wanted to run to the room, taking Devin with her, but she also didn't want to embarrass her new mother-in-law, not to mention Austin and Ben. She talked to a couple of people on her way there and even managed to have her picture taken once or twice, too. By the time she made it to the little office, she was panting and her panties were soaked through. The conference table looked sturdy enough so when she removed her white thong, she sat on it and lifted her dress.

When the door opened, she nearly threw her dress back down, afraid of who it might be. But when Devin started toward her after he clicked the lock closed, she unzipped the tiny zipper at the side of the dress and let her breasts spill out as well.

"Christ! I can't wait." His mouth covered her breast and he sucked hard on the nipple, making her cry out with pleasure. She nearly came up off the table.

Ronnie reached for his pants and had his cock in her hand in record time. He was right; this was going to be fast and dirty. His cock was hard as stone and she was so wet she was sure she was going to leave a stain on the table. When Devin pressed between her thighs, she nearly came when his cock nudged her opening.

"Lay back for me. Lay back and play with your nipples for me while I fuck you. I love to watch you touch yourself; you make my dick hard just thinking about you pulling on your nipples until they're hard and red. That's it, baby, harder."

He surged into her harder with each thrust. Every time he rocked into her, she felt his balls slap against her ass. When he reached down and pressed his thumb over her clit, she came. Lights burst behind her eyelids; the room felt as if it flexed under the power of it. Arching up, she grabbed his shoulders even as another climax ripped over her, hard and fast, rolling along her pussy to the top of her head. She wanted to beg him to stop, it was too much, but she wanted him to fuck her harder because it was not enough. When he suddenly stilled over her, his whole body tense, she felt him come. Throwing back his head, he nearly knocked her off the table with the force of his pounding. Twice more, he rocked and twice more, she came. When Devin finally leaned forward and held himself over her with his good arm, she looked at him.

His face had a slight sheen to it, covered in perspirations like he was. His hair had fallen forward and it was longer than she had ever seen it. It touched along his neck. He lifted his head; she felt the loss of his touch immediately from her breast.

"I love you, Mrs. Grant." His kiss was leisurely and thorough. He explored her mouth with his, using his tongue and lips to get to what he wanted. Ronnie tried to learn from him and was so happy when he groaned at her attempt.

"If you keep this up, baby, I'm going to have to fuck you again. You are much too tempting. I could stay buried right here for the rest of my life."

"It might get a little crowed with our baby growing in there." Ronnie wished she had not said anything. The look of pure horror on his face would have been comical if it hadn't been so serious.

"Did I hurt you? Or her? Christ, Veronica, you should have reminded me. We'll have to stop this kind of sex right now. It'll be just slow and easy sex from now on."

She couldn't help it, she giggled. "Why don't we stop having sex all together? That might be better yet." For a moment, she thought he might agree. "Don't be stupid, Devin, I was kidding. Damon said we can do whatever we have been doing; nothing will harm our baby. He said it got planted that way, it isn't going anywhere now."

"I want a second opinion. He's old, you know. We'll get a young doctor. One who isn't...no, no young doctor. No one is going to be looking at you who's under the age of fifty. When we get back, I expect you to take a two hour nap every day. And you'll start eating—" She kissed him.

It was either that or kill him. It was going to be a long nine months.

Look for book three in
The Grant Brothers Series
Spencer

About the Author

I woke up one morning and decided to give play time to the people in my head who were keeping me awake. Little did I know that they would be so relentless and want their time right now! I wrote for the pure joy of it and to entertain my family and friends. But mostly it was to get more than an hour of sleep without a story playing out. Of course, the more I write, the more they want. So...well, as a result of sleepless days (I work through the night as a gun toting grandma – nope not a vigilantly but an armed security guard) I have lots of stories written.

Hello! My name is Kathi Barton and I'm an author. I have been married to my very best friend Sonny for at times seems several lifetimes – in a good way, honey. And together we have three wonderful children and then the ones we brought into the world - Paul and Dale Barton, Jason and Wendy Barton and Danielle and Ben Conklin. They have given us seven of the greatest treasures on Earth. They don't live at home seven days a week! No, seriously, seven grandchildren – Gavin, Spring, Ben, Trinity, Sarah, Kelly and Kian.

KATHI S BARTON

222